Charles Woodman

The Boys and Girls of the Revolution

Charles Woodman

The Boys and Girls of the Revolution

ISBN/EAN: 9783337234744

Printed in Europe, USA, Canada, Australia, Japan

Cover: Foto ©Andreas Hilbeck / pixelio.de

More available books at **www.hansebooks.com**

THE

BOYS AND GIRLS

OF

THE REVOLUTION.

BY

CHARLES H. WOODMAN.

———

PHILADELPHIA:

J. B. LIPPINCOTT & CO.

1877.

TO

ELLA FARMAN

WHO LEADS THE *WIDE AWAKE* HOST OF YOUNG AMERICANS

THESE SKETCHES OF

THE BOYS AND GIRLS OF THE REVOLUTION

ARE HEARTILY AND GRATEFULLY

DEDICATED.

THE materials for the following sketches have been gathered from a great variety of sources,—from histories, British and American, national and local; from biographies, from the newspapers of the Revolutionary times, and from old journals, diaries, and letters.

As a late gleaner in this rich field, I here record my gratitude to all those through whose faithful labors I am enabled to be "reaping that I did not. sow."

C. H. W.

CONTENTS.

THE

BOYS AND GIRLS

OF THE

REVOLUTION.

THE YOUTH OF 'SEVENTY-SIX.

Young men and maidens, children, and even babes, played an important part in the war for American independence. From every page of its wonderful history some deed of a puny arm stands out from the sturdy blows that fell so thickly for liberty, or some childish prattle is heard amid the roar of cannon and the noise of war. On every field of strife the blood of children mingled with the blood of grandsires.

The first martyr in the cause was a little boy of Boston, whose manly conquest of death was an auspicious opening of the struggle. And in the glorious closing scene at Yorktown, amid the rejoicings of victorious hearts and the tears of conquered heroes, a slight form stepped forth—a mere lad of nineteen—and received the fallen standards of the British Empire.

A*   9

Babes were born in the midst of battle, and
cradled to the sound of guns. Through all that
fierce struggle in Rhode Island two young women,
whose husbands were with the neighboring army
defending their homes, performed all the labor on
the farm, taking their new-born infants with them
to the field: Dorcas Matteson pillowed hers in the
grass, while Emma Aldrich cradled her little one
in the boughs of a tree.

Now and then we catch glimpses of childhood's
innocence and of idyllic pathos in the very thick
of the fight.

On the day after the battle of Brandywine the
British army marched into the village so suddenly
that the people had no warning of their coming.
Two little girls were playing see-saw just at the
entrance to the hamlet, and without a thought of
danger were merrily singing "Yankee Doodle."
At the sudden appearance of the red-coats the terrified children ran screaming to their house, hotly
pursued by the soldiers. The inmates hastily fastened the doors and windows; but the enraged men
burst them open, and rushed in with oaths and
curses. The children's father called loudly for the
commander, who instantly ordered the men back
to the ranks, and the troops marched on.

During the attack on Fort Montgomery, in October, 1777, little Rebecca Rose, seven years of
age, flew around as fast as her feet could carry her,

to save her large stock of rag babies, which she safely hid in a sap-trough, regardless of the balls which screamed about her.

And so the little folk did not escape their share of the suffering which fell so heavily upon all the people. We read horrible tales of the slaughter of the innocents, by exposure or by the hand of the savage Indians, and the oftentimes more brutal white enemies. Many a child was snatched from its slumbers on a sudden assault only to perish in the cold and darkness as its parents fled through the night, or was left in the cradle to be devoured by the flames; or was torn from its mother's arms and dashed in pieces by the inhuman hand of Indian or Tory. One little fellow in Vermont climbed up into the great chimney when his people fled from the whooping savages, and while the half-naked demons sat around the roaring fire they had made, came tumbling down upon the hearth, a suffocated corpse.

When the king's troops were returning from the Concord fight, on the 19th of April, 1775, they entered the house of Mrs. Hannah Adams, whom they found in bed with her new-born child. One of the wretches pulled aside the curtains and threatened to kill them with his bayonet. The poor woman, who was yet too weak to walk, begged for her life. Another soldier then told her she should have time to get out of the house, but the

building must be burned. Clasping her unconscious babe, she crawled out to the corn-house,
where she held the infant to her bosom while the
men set fire to her home. Five little children were
left in the house, and, notwithstanding their terror,
they succeeded in extinguishing the flames after
the troops had departed.

At the attack on Currytown, N. Y., by Indians
and Tories, in July, 1781, Jacob Dievendorff, eleven
years old, and Mary Miller, but ten, were captured.
When the inhabitants fiercely pursued the Indians,
they scalped the children and left them to die. As
the patriots came up to the spot, the lad struggled
through the brush to meet them. His bloody face
made him look like an Indian, and a man aimed
his rifle at him, when another knocked up the muzzle and the ball went into the air. The two children were then taken up and carried toward Fort
Plain. The poor little girl begged piteously for
water, but died the moment she swallowed it. The
lad lived to old age, a monument to the cruelty of
war.

But the tortures of children by Indians and
Tories in beautiful Wyoming and Cherry Valley
would fill a large book with stories of horror.

In many ways the little people were guide-boards
to tell the direction of public feeling, or weather-
vanes which showed the drift of the wind. As the
breach between the countries grew wider and the

war approached, children began to be named after the popular leaders. The famous General Barton, of Rhode Island, called his son, born December 20, 1775, George Washington. He is supposed to be the first of the myriads who have been named for the Father of his country. Mary Vose, in Connecticut, named her triplets George Washington, John Hancock, and Charles Lee. Occasionally some Tory named his child for a leader in the king's cause, and this always produced trouble. Early in 1776 a son of Mr. Edwards, of Stratford, Conn., was baptized to the name of Thomas Gage, commander of the royal troops in America. As soon as this was known an indignation meeting was held by the women of the town. They at once chose a general and other officers, and one hundred and seventy young ladies marched in battle array to pay their compliments to Thomas Gage Edwards, and to bestow a coat of tar and feathers upon his mother. But the father had got word of the danger, and when the petticoat army reached the house he was in the doorway with loaded gun, determined to maintain his rights. The disappointed crusaders retreated, and the baby kept his name. No doubt he was ashamed of it when he grew up, though we do not find that he ever petitioned the legislature for leave to change it.

The sports of the children became filled with

2

war and patriotism. The little imitators caught the watch-words and their meanings, and wove them into their innocent games. When Burgoyne and his officers were entertained by General Schuyler, immediately after the surrender at Saratoga, a number of them occupied one room, and made temporary beds upon the floor. Early in the morning General Schuyler's little son was heard racing up and down the hall, and making the house to ring with his merry laughter. Presently he softly opened the door, and, peering into the room with roguish eyes, screamed, "You are all my prisoners!" then darted back into the hall and laughed loudly at his little joke, which, we are told, stung the British captives with a torturing sense of their unhappy condition.

Some time after his defeat by Colonel Washington, the fierce Tarleton stopped with his cavalry at the house of Dr. Newman. While the royal officers were talking with their host, his little boys were playing battle upon the floor, with red and white kernels of corn for soldiers. The mimic battle of the Cowpens raged furiously. At length they shouted, "Hurrah for Washington! Tarleton runs! Hurrah for Washington!" "See those cursed little rebels!" cried Tarleton, in anger. The British officer was particularly thin-skinned over his defeat at the Cowpens, and once nearly drew his sword upon a lady who reminded him of it.

Bad as he was, he seems to have had a love for children, although he could not bear any more from them than from their elders. He came very near being slain by a little bugler belonging to Colonel Washington's troops.

Boy-and-girl nature, indeed, seems to have been the same one hundred years ago that it is now. Keen-witted, wide awake, intensely active, always on hand when any excitement was afoot,—the young patriots are seen at every turn of revolutionary affairs. We find them active at the Boston massacre, and in the burning of effigies in South Carolina. The streets of the cities swarmed with them; they were irrepressible, and formed an element which had to be taken into account by both friends and foes.

As Lord Percy marched his troops through Roxbury to the Concord fight, the band played "Yankee Doodle," in derision of the Yankee. A little boy in the street cut such ridiculous antics that Lord Percy asked him why he was so merry. "To think how you will dance by and by to 'Chevy Chase,'" said the sharp lad; and the earl felt it keenly.

After the brilliant capture of General Prescott, in Rhode Island, by a handful of patriots, the English officers were very sore and crestfallen. The old general was universally hated on the island, and the people were rejoiced to be rid of his tyr-

anny. But the children fathomed the chagrin of
the British officers, and entered into a ludicrous
conspiracy to aggravate their grief. The youngsters took every occasion to throw themselves in
the way of their oppressors, when they would hold
their handkerchiefs to their eyes, make the most
horrible faces, and howl so lugubriously that the
toughest heroes were fairly driven from the field.

Some witty man composed a song on this capture of Prescott, which the young lads used to sing
in hearing of the English officers, who did not
relish its keen ridicule and sarcasm.

One night, after General Prescott had been ex-
changed and returned to his army at Newport, in
the midst of a great carousal, the old soldier called
for a song. As none of the half-drunken officers
seemed able to oblige him, some one said, "There
is a boy in the kitchen who is a famous singer."
The general sent for him, and ordered him to sing.
The little fellow said he did not know anything
"except the one about Barton taking old Prescott,"
and immediately struck off into the hated song,
which he sang with hearty feeling through all its
length. The tyrannical old general enjoyed the
joke so well that he praised the lad's voice and
gave him half a crown.

When Ethan Allen set forth in wrath to thrash
the Tory printer Rivington, of New York, who
had been abusing the patriots in his paper, a great

crowd of boys gathered around the tall figure in tarnished regimentals, mammoth cocked hat, and enormous long-sword clanging on the stones at every step, and loudly cheered the hero on, for they saw by his face that there was fun of some kind ahead. When the angry man strode into the office, the boys climbed over one another on the steps and flattened their noses against the glass door, peering in, and hooting and yelling as if it were a dog-fight. But no fight came off, and the disappointed youngsters dispersed, intensely disgusted with Ethan Allen for settling his quarrel over a bottle of Madeira.

It was a boy, too, who was the origin of the great Doctor's Mob, in New York, in 1778.

Lads who were too young to bear arms found ways enough in which to show their zeal and do their best for the cause of liberty. They worked in the trenches, they drove the teams when fortifications were built, they acted as scouts and guides. One of the best accounts we have of the American army on Dorchester Heights was written by Jeremiah Boies, who, being then but eleven years of age, tended his father's horses through all that terrible night of labor and anxiety when the British attack from Boston was hourly expected.

On that eventful morning in April, 1775, while Colonel Barrett was leading his minute-men to meet the British attack at Concord, his little grand-

2*

son, fourteen years old, was working with all the other village lads to remove the stores of powder which the king's troops had come out to capture, loading them into ox-teams, with a lad posted each side of the cattle to goad them into a trot. The boys had concealed all the stores in the woods and had returned to the village to make cartridges before the British were driven back.

Just as Fort Montgomery surrendered to the British assault, Beverly Garrison, a lad of fourteen, was teaming a large cannon to the outworks, and, refusing to run away from his team, he was captured.

Ethan Allen might never have made his famous capture of Fort Ticonderoga had he not been helped by a boy. Allen had but a few men, and must take the place by stratagem, not force. It was necessary to know how to enter the fortress and how to reach the officers' quarters. The colonel applied to a neighboring farmer named Beman for a guide. The farmer offered him his son Nathan a small lad who spent his time playing with the boys of the garrison, and so knew every secret passage within the fort. Day was beginning to dawn as Allen took the lad's hand and returned to his troops. Only eighty-three men had yet crossed the lake; but there was no time to wait, and, after a short speech to his followers, the gallant officer led them up the heights, guided by little Nathan, to the sally-port. The first sentinel fled, the second was captured, and the patriots, piloted by the brave lad, rushed to the commandant's quarters. The fort was ours.

On nearly every battle-field of the war we find boys who, too young to be enrolled in the army, were fighting on their own account and in their own way.

While General Wilkinson, who was Gates's adjutant-general, was pursuing the flying enemy at Saratoga, he heard a feeble voice from the grass crying, "Protect me, sir, from that boy!" Reining in his horse, the general saw a small lad taking cool aim with a musket at a wounded British officer, who was lying under a fence. The boy was ordered off by the general, who then discovered the wounded man to be Major Ackland, one of the noblest of the king's officers.

Lieutenant-Colonel Simcoe, a famous partisan officer, commanding the Queen's Rangers, tells us that he himself was barely saved from being bayoneted by a little boy as he lay wounded upon the field where he was captured.

In every village of the country the young lads formed military companies and trained with wooden guns. One of these mimic companies once saved a terrible massacre. The dreaded Indian chieftain Brandt led his savage followers stealthily through the woods to make a descent upon the settlement in Cherry Valley. As he approached the place, he climbed a neighboring peak to reconnoitre. Looking down upon the fort, he saw a large company of boys drilling with such precision that he thought they must be regular soldiers, and so he retreated to wait for a more favorable time.

While the British held Rhode Island the inhabitants suffered greatly from the plundering enemy. At last their depredations became unbearable, and, as all the men were with the American army, the boys all along the shore formed into companies to protect their parents' property. They did good service, and acted with great bravery, although the oldest of them was only sixteen. There was another boy-company in Bristol; and when the British burned the town these little lads stood gallantly at their posts and saved the place from total destruction.

At the British descent upon Connecticut, the Yale College boys turned out in defense, led by the brave young Aaron Burr.

Meanwhile, the girls were not idle, but did famous service, especially as scouts and spies. When the war was carried into the Southern States, it became unusually fierce and bitter, for it was a war between neighbors and families. The Tory feeling was very strong, and, while the royal army was near, the patriots of the neighborhood could not stay at home, but were forced to conceal themselves in the woods and swamps. This was called "lying out." At such times the young girls were of great service. They carried food to their fathers and kept them informed of affairs, often creeping to them at the dead of night, always at the risk of their own lives and of betraying the hiding-places of their dear ones.

Their sex gave them many advantages over their brothers, and they used their liberty, as their gentle hearts led them, to soothe the suffering and help the afflicted. To many a battle-field and prison did the women and girls bring light and comfort. When Dr. Platt was imprisoned in New York, his young daughter Dorothea was so persistent in her journeys to Sir Henry Clinton, and in her pleadings with him, that this officer was finally glad to release his captive.

Colonel Smith was kept in the same prison under the brutal Cunningham, and his daughter Hannah sacrificed herself in her attempts to get him set free, for she caught such a cold from the exposure of her long night-tramps in bitter weather that she became incurably deaf.

The noble spirit and the noble deeds of the youth of '76 sprang largely from the training of the parents, whose hearts were run in the antique mould. Fathers, on their death-beds, consecrated their children to the holy work, and mothers' hands armed them and sent them forth.

An old man had five sons in the battle of Bennington. He was told that one of them had been unfortunate. "What!" cried he, in agony, "has he misbehaved? Did he desert his post or shrink from the charge?" "Worse than that," was the reply; "he was slain, but fighting nobly." "Then I am satisfied. Bring him to me." And the corpse was laid at the father's feet. He gently wiped the blood from the wound and exclaimed, through tears, "This is the happiest day of my life, to know that my five sons fought nobly for freedom, though one has fallen in the conflict."

A Connecticut mother sent out her sons to battle, the youngest but fourteen years of age. Presently he returned, as he could get no musket. "Go back, my son!" cried the heroic mother; "go into battle and *take* a gun from the enemy."

"Alick," said Mrs. Haynes, of North Carolina, as she equipped her son, a mere boy, for the battle of Rocky Mount, "Alick, now fight like a man. *Don't* be a coward!"

Just after the bloody fight at Hanging Rock, the venerable Mrs. Gaston was told that three of her sons lay dead upon the field. "I grieve for their loss," she calmly replied; "but they could not have died in a better cause." Her grandsons were about her knees, and she would not shed a tear.

The battle of King's Mountain caused Cornwallis to retreat toward Camden. On the march he stopped a night on Wilson's plantation, near Steel Creek. The earl and the brutal Tarleton entered the house, and, finding Mrs. Wilson alone, asked for her family. Husband and sons were with Sumter. Cornwallis endeavored, by brilliant promises, to win the good woman's influence for the king. He told her that he had just captured her husband and eldest son (which was true), and that if she would bring her family to the royal service her loved ones should be liberated and promoted to rank and power. "Sir," said this noble mother, "I have seven· sons now bearing arms; my seventh son, who is only fifteen years of age, I yesterday sent to join his brothers in Sumter's army. Now, sir, sooner than see one of my family turn back from the glorious work I would take these *boys*"—and she pointed to three or four little fellows—"and enlist myself under Sumter's banner, and show my husband and sons how to fight, and, if necessary, to *die* for their country!"

Such training was sure to fill the children with the spirit of self-sacrifice, devotion, and courage; and this spirit was, indeed, manifested by all classes of youth, from infancy to mature years.

A most touching example was given in North Carolina, before the outbreak of the war, when the "Regulators" were beginning their struggle against tyranny. Six of these patriots were at one time captured and condemned to death. One, named Messer, had a wife and a family of young children. His wife went to Governor Tryon, who was called " the Great Wolf," and, falling on her knees, begged for her husband's life. The governor would not heed her. Then her little son, seven years old, clasped the Great Wolf's knees and besought that *he* might be hanged instead of his father. "What do you want to be hanged for?" asked the brutal man. " Because if you hang my father, my mother will die and all of us will perish." But tears and misery could not move this wicked ruler, and the poor father was hung.

And the girls showed the home influences as plainly as their brothers. A certain little maiden of Charleston chanced to hear a British officer speak contemptuously of General Marion. She quickly snatched off her shoe and flung it in his face, crying, " Go, coward, and meet him !"

Early in the war the young ladies of Amelia County, Virginia, solemnly agreed among themselves not to permit any love-making from any person, however wealthy or high in station, unless he had served in the American army long enough to prove both his patriotism and his valor. The boys in that part of the county all went to the war.

At Kinderhook, New York, a lot of girls were having a merry quilting frolic one evening, when a young man walked in, and soon began to sneer at

Congress and the army, for he was a Tory. The patriotic girls first tried to silence him with argument, but, becoming exasperated, concluded to try a more effective method. They suddenly fell upon the presumptuous wretch, stripped him to the waist, covered him with molasses for tar, and, instead of feathers, took the downy tops of flags, which grew in the meadows, and gave him a heavy coat. Then they turned him out.

While the girls thus took care of the enemies at home, their brothers who were old enough to bear arms faced the enemy on the field. And in those times of our country's need the boys did not wait to be very old. Hundreds of them enlisted at the age of fourteen. A large part of our force at Bunker Hill were mere lads, and one-third of the heroic defenders of Fort Mifflin were under sixteen. Stephen Martindale, afterwards a colonel in the war of 1812, was a lad of sixteen, weighing only sixty-six pounds, when he fought all through the battle of Bennington.

Very many of the officers of our army were in their teens, and numbers of them rose to eminence before they had attained to years of manhood. Uzal Knapp was an officer of Washington's Life-Guard when eighteen, and at the same age William Colfax had the proud honor of being commander of this noble body of gallant soldiers. Between young Colfax and General Washington there arose

B   3

a strong attachment, and the great man often shared his tent and table with his youthful friend.

Much of the lustre that shines upon us across the century's space flows from the deeds of youth. The history of the American Revolution is largely the history of young men.

THE FIRST MARTYR.

In the opening of the year 1770 Boston was a sleeping volcano. The Stamp Act had been repealed, but the royal government still imposed a tax on several articles of daily use, among which was the universal favorite—tea. Worse than all this, the quiet old town had been turned into a garrison. Two regiments of British soldiers had been sent here to overawe the people and to impress them with the love and mercy of the mother-country. If, a peaceable citizen took his wife and children by the hand for an hour's stroll through the streets, he was met at every corner by the challenge of the British sentry; if he went upon the Common to get the soft air from the country, he found only a drill-ground for British troops; and when he turned to the wharves for the sea-breeze, he was threatened by the gaping mouths of British cannon from the British ships at anchor in the harbor.

Restricted in their diet, and confined in their movements, the good people of Boston felt that

27

they were fast becoming slaves. They might have drank tea, to be sure, but they were too high-spirited to swallow it when sweetened with British taxes; and although they were free to move to and fro, they held their freedom subject to the pleasure of a British tyrant, and exercised it daily in the face of British insults.

The patriots of Boston and the neighboring towns had sworn to drink no tea while the tax continued, nor would they deal with the merchants who imported the hated, yet longed-for, herb. In 1768 there were fifteen hundred families in Boston which had given up their favorite drink, while all the students of Harvard College but four had joined the self-denying throng. On the 9th of February, 1770, the women of Boston met together, and the names of three hundred mothers of families were added to those who had forsworn the use of tea. The spirit that moved the parents during these trying scenes was at work in the hearts of their children. Three days after the mothers' meeting, the daughters arose in indignation and subscribed by hundreds to the following vow:

"We, the daughters of those patriots who have, and do now, appear for the public interest, and in that principally regard their posterity,—as such, do with pleasure engage with them in denying ourselves the drinking of foreign tea, in hopes to frustrate a plan which tends to deprive a whole community of all that is valuable in life."

Meanwhile, the presence of British soldiers grew more irksome and dangerous. The troops looked upon the people with scorn, and the people hated their oppressors. Street-fights between the parties became common, and the civil and military authorities were often in collision. No quarters could be hired for the troops, and they forcibly seized such buildings as they needed. They built a guardhouse, and the people tore it down. They were fond of flourishing their weapons in the streets and abusing the people, while the citizens did not hide their hatred and bitterness.

This bitterness was increased by the arrest of a great favorite of the people, John Hancock, and by the terrible beating of another favorite, James Otis, in a coffee-house.

During all these eventful days the boys of Boston were wide awake. They heard the growing troubles discussed at their fathers' tables, and drank in the spirit of independence with every breath they drew. As they passed to and from their schools, or played on the Common and in the streets, they were often abused by the British soldiers, and were quick to repay their insults in the manifold ways which boys' genius can invent. They heard everything, saw everything, and were everywhere active. Where was ever an affray in

3*

which the ubiquitous boy did not take a part? A quarrel between a soldier and a citizen would bring the boys swarming from every lane and alley. They even fought hand-to-hand with the troops on the Common. Untameable, irrepressible, omnipresent, the jibes and jeers and antics of the lads of Boston were the spirit of '76 run mad. What their fathers whispered in secret they shouted aloud in the streets, and the insults which the parents quietly endured were resented by their children with a boy's utter recklessness of courage. And so it fitly came to pass that when the sleeping volcano was aroused, the vent through which the fiery storm should burst was opened by a boy's small hand.

Although the patriots would not drink the taxed tea, there were yet five merchants in Boston who persisted in importing it for the use of the British and their sympathizers in the town. The names of these traders were regularly printed in the papers, as hostile to the liberties of their country. One of them was Theophilus Lillie, whose store was at the North End, near Mr. Pemberton's church.

One forenoon—it was the 22d of February—a crowd of boys and children came down the street with shouts and laughter, bearing a pole crowned with a large board. On the board, which was covered with paper, were displayed the figures of four of the tea-importing merchants, and one end was rudely cut into the shape of a hand, with the forefinger outstretched. When the merry procession reached the store of Theophilus Lillie, the boys planted the pole in the middle of the street, with the finger pointing toward Lillie's shop. Then the children shouted and capered around, hugely enjoying the sport they were having at the expense of the obnoxious merchant.

Among these lads was Christopher Snyder, a little fellow but eleven years of age. His parents were honest, industrious, worthy people, but they were poor, and had placed their child as a servant in the family of Madame Apthorp. The boy was a favorite among his fellows, active in all sports, merry and generous in his disposition. He was thoughtful, too, beyond his years, and showed a brave and manly heart that promised well for his future. This was a play-day with him, and, having joined his comrades, he tripped along in high glee, foremost in the fun. Not a thought of evil darkened his young and happy heart. Beside him ran little Christopher Gore, whose sun was rising instead of going into night, and who was destined to become a governor of his native State.

The noise soon collected a crowd of people, mostly boys, who entered heartily into the fun, and cheered loudly at the joke. But there was one man present who looked upon the show with different feelings. This was Ebenezer Richard-

son, who was said to be a custom-house officer
and an informer. He soon grew angry at the
daring insult to his friend, and seeing a country-
man driving by with his cart, shouted to him to
ride the pole down. But the farmer was a good
patriot, and enjoyed the sport too well to be willing to spoil it himself. The boys now shouted
the louder, and Richardson grew more enraged
than ever. Seeing a lumbering charcoal cart come
down the street, he tried to get the driver to run
against the pole and knock it down.

But the boys' spirit was now aroused, and they
crowded around their sign-board to defend it
against assault. The charcoal-man refused to in-
terfere, and drove off amid the cheers of the multitude.

It is easy to excite boys to desperation. What
they had begun in sport they now resolved to
carry through in earnest. They had set up their
idol, and they were ready to fight for its safety.
They hooted at Richardson, and jostled against
him until his ears tingled and his heart boiled at
their jeers. He started toward his house, which
was near by, followed by the children still yelling
in derision.

At this moment four well-known citizens came
along, and Richardson abused them with rough
words, shouting, " Perjury ! perjury !" at the top
of his voice. The crowd now broke into a storm

of rage, screaming at the man and pelting him
with dirt and stones. He rushed into his house
and fastened the door. But the boys had no idea
of attacking him, and had already turned back to
their sign-board with hilarious shouts, when Richardson threw up his window and pointed a gun
toward the crowd.

"I'll make the place too hot for some of you
before night!" he cried.

Yells of derision from the boys answered this
threat.

"I'll make a lane through you if you don't go
away!" screamed the man.

The crowd replied with a shower of stones.

Then the gun blazed from the window, and terrible shrieks went up from the wild tumult below.

"Who's hit? who is it?" cried the boys,
surging back and forth in confusion. Two young
voices were screaming in agony.

"It's Snyder! Chris Snyder!" shouted some.

"And Chris Gore, too!" cried others. "Here,
boys! help!"

All crowded around the two lads, who were
on the ground writhing and shrieking with pain.
Young Gore was shot in one hand and both thighs,
but little Christopher Snyder was terribly mangled.
Soon the poor boys' screams died away to moans,
and, lifting the sufferers from the ground, the crowd
moved slowly away with the sorrowful burden.

B*

As the throng turned away, a squad of men burst into the meeting-house near by, and, leaping upon the bell-rope, rang out with fierce energy the peals for fire. Immediately a stream of people poured in from every quarter.

"Fire! fire! Where is the fire?" cried the gathering crowd.

But the great bell spoke a word far more appalling than "fire."

"Murder! murder!" it hurled out over the startled town, till every ear rung with the awful sound and every heart felt the blows of the iron tongue.

Terrible was the wrath of the multitude when they gathered about the innocent blood. Fathers were there who knew not but it was the life of their own children appealing to them so piteously from the stones of the street. With a wild shout the throng rushed upon the house of the murderer and thundered at the door. They attacked the building on all sides; soon a door gave way, and the enraged crowd poured in. They found the murderer trembling for his life. Beside him was another man armed with a gun. The men were captured, and the gun was examined. It contained a heavy charge of powder, and one hundred and seventy-nine goose-shot. This added fuel to the burning hearts.

The two prisoners were caught up, and the wild

storm swept on to the magistrate's, thence to Faneuil Hall, where the prisoners were examined, and then to the jail, which they barely reached with their lives.

Meanwhile, amid tears and sobs, the mourning boys carried their comrades on. The little sufferer had regained his self-control, and he bore bravely his agony, without murmur or moan. Men crowded about the sorrowing throng at every step,—gazed a moment into the innocent child-face and at the gaping wound that cried for vengeance,—thought of their own dear boys whose lives were no longer safe, and rushed away to the scene of strife, flaming with grief and rage. The mourning cries of the children entered the houses along the way. From hastily-opened windows peered many a mother's face, whose tender tears fell freely on the stones below, and who turned away to fold her own loved flock more closely to her fearful heart.

Little Snyder had been living with Madam Apthorp, but at this awful hour all hearts turned to the stricken parents, and to their home the dying child was borne.

The boys entered Frog Lane, now Boylston Street, and laid the mangled son in the mother's arms. A doctor came at once, but the wounds were mortal, and no skill could save the lad. Eleven large swan-shot were taken from the little fellow's flesh. In his pocket were found several pieces of heroic writing which he loved to read, among them Wolfe's "Summit of Human Glory."

From his wounding to his death he displayed a courage and nobility of spirit marvelous in one so young. When carried into the house, he met his distracted mother with a smile. He answered clearly and calmly the many questions of the physician. To the clergyman who often prayed with him, he expressed the keenest gratitude and the utmost willingness to meet the King of Terrors. His agony was excruciating, yet of the multitude that filled the house, he alone neither sobbed nor moaned. Gradually the young life sank away, and when the second evening fell upon the stricken home the lad's spirit went unto the God who loves justice and hates tyranny.

The news of Snyder's death flew wildly through the town. All classes of people felt the grief to be their own. The boy was looked upon as a hero who had fallen in the cause of liberty, and great preparations were made to honor him with a public funeral.

On Monday, the 26th of February, a vast concourse, of all ages and ranks, assembled around the Liberty Tree which stood opposite Frog Lane. On this sacred tree was nailed a board, inscribed, "Thou shalt take no satisfaction for the life of a murderer; he shall surely be put to death."

The coffin holding the poor lad's body was brought out and set down under the tree, which bent its branches over it in solemn blessing. On the foot of the coffin were the words, "*Latet anguis in herba;*" on the sides was written, "*Haeret lateri lethalis arundo;*" and at the head the startling words, "*Innocentia nusquam tuta,*" assuring every parent's heart that "innocence itself is not safe." In the midst of weeping and the cries of many mothers the procession formed. Five hundred children marched in couples at the head. Then came the bier, borne by six of the murdered boy's playfellows, chosen by his parents for this sad and holy work. After the bier moved heavily the stricken hearts and their sorrowing friends. Then followed thirteen hundred citizens on foot, and great numbers of chariots and chaises closed the mournful pageant.

As the procession moved forward, the bells of Boston sobbed through the hushed air, and in all the neighboring towns every church-steeple sounded the universal grief.

Slowly the imposing array wound on to the burying-place in the Common, where, 'mid the awful stillness broken only by the moans of mothers, the fierce beatings of fathers' hearts, and the solemn words of the service, was laid the consecrated body of the boy who was the first martyr in the cause of American independence.

BOYS IN THE BOSTON MASSACRE.

THE thrill of horror and grief that moved the patriot hearts of Boston at the murder of Christopher Snyder, made the people more sensitive than ever to the presence and insults of the British troops. The breach between the citizens and the soldiery daily widened, and both parties became more intolerant in their actions.

The boys, especially, resented the murder of their comrade. The heart of every lad burned with hatred of the brutal soldiers who wreaked upon the children the malice they dared not always show to the fathers. The boys' sports were interrupted, their play-grounds invaded,—and many a little fellow ran home in tears of pain from the blow of some uniformed ruffian. It is not in boy's nature to meekly bear abuse. The lads of Boston repaid their tormentors as best they could, —annoying them by ingenious tricks, snow-balling them in the street, and hooting after them in that aggravating manner which only a boy can use to perfection.

The neighborhood of the barracks was, of course, the scene of frequent collisions. The Fourteenth Regiment was quartered in Murray's barracks, on Brattle Street, nearly opposite the covered passage which opens into Cornhill. The Twenty-ninth was stationed in Water Street, and near several large ropewalks, where many boys and young men were employed. In the first week of March two soldiers met one of these young ropemakers, and provoked him so much that he sprang upon them and knocked them both flat. The soldiers sneaked off to their barracks boiling with rage, shame, and revenge. On the forenoon of Friday, the 3d of March, a number of the British came to John Gray's ropewalk, flourishing swords and clubs, and shouting threats to the busy workers within. The boys and young men only laughed at the angry soldiers and mocked at them with jeers. Then the leader of the British ruffians challenged any one to single combat. One of the ropemakers stepped out, beat the boastful soldier unmercifully in fair fight, took his sword away, and drove him off. He soon came back with nearly a dozen comrades. The ropewalk boys rushed out, pounced upon the red-coats, and once more chased them out of sight. Again they came back, this time with nearly forty soldiers, determined to wipe out their disgrace. A fierce hand-to-hand fight with swords and bludgeons brought

victory to the soldiers, who were three to one.
Many were badly wounded on both sides, and the
combatants separated with feelings of the bitterest
hatred and revenge. Such feelings cannot long
lie quiet.

On Monday, the 5th, the snow fell steadily
through the day. Toward evening the sky cleared,
and as darkness gathered in the streets the moon
came brightly forth to look upon a dreadful night's
work. A spirit of unrest and of foreboding
haunted all the glimmering streets of the quiet
town. Here and there were groups of citizens,
clustering closely together, and talking in low and
troubled tones. Dark figures flitted noiselessly
to and fro with all the mysteriousness of ghostly
visitants. At times the still, calm air was startled
by wild shouts, as gangs of soldiers rushed with
curses through the streets. Following these rioters
with their eyes, the anxious citizens saw flashing
gleams amid the groups, as the moonlight revealed the soldiers' weapons.

There was reason, then, for every troubled face.
The forebodings deepened into fears, and soon became sharp certainty.

Through all the day the soldiers had been busy
among their friends, warning them to keep in-doors
that night. They had armed themselves with
swords and clubs, and were now abroad with desperate designs.

In one place a crowd of boys had gathered; the soldiers, dashing through them, struck right and left with sticks and cutlasses.

The nine o'clock clangs of the Old South bell had scarcely died upon the air when four youths came down Cornhill, separating at the corner, on the way to their homes. Two of the boys, Edward Archbald and William Merchant, crossed the street and entered Boylston's Alley. Here was posted a British sentry, who was swinging an enormous broadsword over his head and hacking fire from the walls. Beside him stood a mean-looking Irishman, armed with a huge bludgeon. As the lads passed down the alley the sentry gave the challenge, but the two kept on without noticing the hated sound. The sentinel flourished his broadsword before them, and brought it down furiously upon the wall. Archbald shouted to his comrade to look out for the sword. The soldier sprang forward and struck the first lad heavily on the arm, then turned quickly and made a desperate lunge at Merchant. The sword passed through his clothes and tore the skin under the arm-pit. The boy rallied and struck the sentry with a stick he carried in his hand. They fell to scuffling, and the cowardly Irishman ran off to the barracks for help. Two soldiers came back, one armed with a shovel and the other with tongs. The fellow with the tongs leaped at Archbald, who turned and ran;

4*

but the soldier caught him by the collar and beat him terribly over the head.   The screams and curses now brought in people from the street, and a little fellow named John Hicks hurled his light weight so impetuously against the soldier as to knock him down.   The boy let the great coward get up, however, then sprang upon him like a cat. The noise of the fight had reached the quick ears of all the lads in the neighborhood, who came pouring into the alley, eager for the fun.   They fell furiously upon the red-coats and drove them into the barracks.   The boys now blockaded the doors, cheering and yelling like so many demons. The maddened soldiers soon rushed out in numbers, armed with clubs, cutlasses, and bayonets. They charged upon the lads, who held their ground bravely, and for a while the battle was fierce.   But bare fists were no match for bare steel, and the plucky youngsters gradually fell back, while the red-coats rushed on toward Dock Square.

A sailor from Wellfleet named Atwood was just entering the alley; leaping back in amazement, he cried, "Do you mean to murder the people?" "Yes, by ——, root and branch!" was the awful answer, followed by a blow from a heavy club. Atwood turned to flee, when another stroke cut him open to the bone.

"Where are the Yankee boogers?   Where are

the cowards?" yelled the soldiers, as they sprang into the square.

Two officers now came upon the scene. "What is the matter?" cried Atwood. "You'll see by and by," was the answer.

The officers ordered the men to the barracks, and they reluctantly turned back. The alley was now filled with an excited throng. A boy stood near the entrance with a piece of barrel stave in his hand. "Here is one of 'em!" shouted the retreating soldiers; and they rushed forward to set upon him. The brave lad brandished his stick, and the British heroes turned aside and passed him by.

A little fellow came running along, crying loudly, with his hand to his poor, bruised head, "Oh! I'm killed! I'm killed!" "Get out of the way, you cursed little rascal!" yelled an officer.

A soldier ran out of the barracks, and kneeling on one knee, at the end of the alley, leveled his musket and shouted, with an oath, "I'll make a lane through you all!" The officer knocked up his gun, and pushed the villain toward the barrack's steps. Here Ensign Maul was wildly screaming, "Turn out, and I'll stand by you! Kill 'em! stick 'em! knock 'em down! run your bayonets through 'em!"

The soldier again came out, and prepared to fire, but his musket was snatched away. The troops now ran into the barracks, hotly pursued by the infuriated mob.

Suddenly a strong cry rang above the clamor, "Town born, turn out! town born, turn out!"

"Fire! fire! fire!" came from all quarters.

In a moment the bells pealed out upon the night with furious energy.

The clamor was now appalling. The throng was rapidly growing in numbers and fierceness, when a large, tall man lifted himself above the crowd. His gallant figure, red cloak, and flowing white wig attracted immediate attention. The mob paused in their assault upon the barracks. The stranger made a short speech, while some listened and others were tearing up the stalls in the market for clubs and cudgels.

Soon there were wild, confused shouts. "Home! home!" cried some. "Hurrah for the main guard! To the main guard! there's the nest!" yelled others. "Let's kill the sentry and attack the main guard!"

The wild mob of men and boys rushed like a whirlwind toward King Street, to attack the guard.

The bells were flinging their fire-peals over all the town; the streets were filled with excited multitudes,—maddened, frightened, cursing, crying.

As the mob entered King Street, another crowd poured in from the south end.

Before the custom-house paced a sentry.

"There's the soldier who knocked me down the other day!" cried a little boy, running up to the steps.

"Kill him! kill him! knock him down!" shouted the mob; and about twenty boys rushed upon the sentinel, who retreated up the steps. He began to load his musket, while the youngsters pelted him with snow-balls, lumps of ice, and sticks of wood. The soldier rammed home his ball.

"Fire! fire if you dare!" taunted the crowd.

The boys sprang up the steps.

The poor sentry banged at the door of the custom-house, and shouted to be let in. No one came to his aid. The infuriated boys now jammed him against the wall. He struck at them with his bayonet, pricking several, and called loudly for the main guard.

At this moment a British dandy, Captain Goldfinch, was seen on the street. A barber's lad spied him, and screamed, "There goes a mean fellow, who has not paid my master for dressing his hair!"

On this the sentinel stepped out and struck the boy a staggering blow with his musket.

The soldier was sensitive on this point. He had himself been shaved by the quarter at a shop kept by Piermont, who allowed his little apprentice to have the pay. The boy had persistently dunned the red-coat, but without success, and the last time he presented the bill the soldier knocked him down.

"Why don't you fire?" yelled the crowd to the frightened sentry.

"The lobster dares not fire!"

They made another rush upon him.

"Stand off!" he cried, as he wielded his bayonet; but the boys had lost all fear.

"Ho! main guard!" roared the soldier. "Main guard to the rescue!"

Just then a man rushed into the guard-house, screaming, "They are killing the sentinel! Turn out the guard!"

A squad of soldiers with fixed bayonets came out, led by a corporal, and followed by Captain Preston with drawn sword.

"Make way!" they cried, thrusting their bayonets before to clear a path.

The men were posted in a semicircle before the custom-house. As the crowd pressed on them they wielded their bayonets fiercely. The boys now assailed them with snow-balls, and sticks were hurled from the dense throng.

Captain Preston was fearfully agitated. The fury of the mob increased.

"Load and prime!" cried the captain to his men.

"You are not going to fire?" asked some citizens of the officer.

"Not unless I am compelled to," said Preston.

A gentleman rushed up and seized him by the coat. "For God's sake, take your men back again!

If they fire, your life must answer for the consequences."

"I know what I am about," answered Preston,
roughly; but the color had all gone from his face.

Ten or a dozen from the crowd, armed with
sticks, started out cheering, and passed before the
soldiers, knocking down their muskets, and shouting, "You're cowardly rascals for bringing arms
against naked men.* Put down your guns and
we're ready for you!"

The small boys all cheered and yelled; they
gave another volley of snow-balls and sticks.
"Come on, you rascals!" they screamed. "Come
on, you bloody-backs! you lobster scoundrels!"
"Fire if you dare! you dare not fire!"

There was now a great uproar toward Cornhill.
A crowd of sailors and others, led by Crispus
Attucks, a mulatto, or half-breed, came rushing toward the guard-house, yelling, "Attack the
main guard! Strike at the root! This is the
nest!"

But seeing the tumult by the custom-house,
the new-comers turned aside and reinforced the
throng around the soldiers. Here the boys were
growing more daring and reckless. A fresh onslaught was made. One fellow struck the musket
of a soldier, Montgomery. The soldier drew back,
leveled his gun, and fired. Crispus Attucks fell.

The tumult rose to a deafening pitch. Above

all was heard the fatal order, " Fire ! be the consequences what they may !"

The muskets blazed out: a dozen men fell;
shrieks and yells rent the air; the crowd were fired
upon from the windows of the custom-house ; a
sudden fear seized the throng: it broke and fled in
all directions.

But thousands were pouring into King Street
from every quarter.   The tides met; the flood-
tide was the strongest, and the wave of infuriated
humanity again swept down upon the troops.

The bells were now ringing the alarm through
the whole town.   On every hand were heard
drums beating, while far and near rose a fearful
cry,—

" To arms ! to arms !   Turn out with your guns,
every man !"

Some of the crowd came on to pick up the dead
and wounded.   The soldiers leveled their muskets,
but the captain knocked them up and commanded
the men to hold.

The regimental drums had also beat to arms.
The soldiers of the Fourteenth rushed out, eager
for vengeance, crying, " This is our time !"

The Twenty-ninth turned out in full force.
Captain Preston formed the men in platoons, and
waited for the commanding officers.

Many prominent citizens were now on the
ground, interposing to disarm the soldiers' hatred

and the people's fury. The throng listened, and became calmer.

Lieutenant-Governor Hutchinson, and Colonel Carr, of the Twenty-ninth, now met at the head of the troops. An appeal was made to these officers to withdraw the soldiers. They hesitated. The men were in platoons ready to fire. The enraged patriots insisted upon their demand. Reluctantly the troops were ordered to shoulder arms and march to the barracks. The multitude quietly dispersed, while one hundred citizens, among them some of the most influential patriots, remained all night to guard the peace of the town.

After the storm! A calm,—but the calmness of fear, of deep determination, of death.

Captain Preston hid himself. The soldiers crowded together in the barracks in gloom. They felt a fearful web was weaving around them; they knew their day of triumph was over; the hour of retribution had come.

The hearts of the patriots went down into the valley of death and gazed upon a frightful scene; then mounted in righteous wrath and invincible determination to that glorious height whence they cease not to shine down upon us to the present day.

The street was strewn with slain and mangled. Samuel Gray lay dead, his skull horribly crushed. Crispus Attucks had poured out his fierce spirit through two bullet-wounds in his breast. James

c   5

Caldwell lay with cold, upturned face, covered with blood, which called more eloquently for vengeance than could his tongue have cried if living. Others were wounded, some fatally.

As the search went on, the grief and horror grew. Here was a slight, frail form. Turn him over! Ah, they knew him! Samuel Maverick, but seventeen years of age, the son of a poor widow, whose heart would now be fully desolate. The lad was breathing, but the end was sure. He died in a few hours. Still another! Christopher Monk, seventeen, terribly torn by balls; yet he finally recovered. The next, too, was a lad of the same age: John Clark, of Medford, an apprentice in town. He was borne away tenderly and with tears, for he was desperately wounded and close to death. He was saved, however, against all hopes. One other little fellow, David Parker, was found with a ball in his hip; the rest of the sufferers were men.

Away from this gloom and horror the citizens turned, with one resolve filling every breast. The examination of witnesses was already going on; officers of the law were searching for Captain Preston; in the Council-chamber met a solemn conclave.

Preston could not be found, but about three o'clock in the morning he came and surrendered himself. The soldiers who fired on the people were taken, and cast into jail.

At daylight the whole town was afoot. Throngs filled the streets, all tending toward Faneuil Hall. At eleven o'clock the town-meeting was held. It was a solemn hour. Dr. Cooper lifted up a prayer of intense power. Then the events of the night were discussed. There was but one decision; it was not only unanimous, it was irrevocable.

Fifteen men, led by Samuel Adams, were sent to Lieutenant-Governor Hutchinson to demand the instant removal of the troops from the town. He replied that he had no power over the military.

The throng was so vast that the meeting, meanwhile, adjourned to the Old South Church. Presently a great cry arose from the street,—

"Make way for the committee!"

They entered the church. Every eye was bent upon the noble face of Samuel Adams. Amid profound stillness the report was given. It would not do. The troops *must* be removed. A new committee of seven was chosen, to carry back Boston's final message. Here were great men,—Adams, Hancock, Warren,—the power of Boston was concentrated here.

They found the chief magistrate in the Council-chamber. Adams delivered the demand.

"The troops are not subject to my authority; I have no power to remove them," was the reply.

Then rose the giant heart of Samuel Adams. Majestically erect, with outstretched arm, he hurled

the might of his freeman's soul against the power
of tyranny.   His logic, his passion, were irresistible.
"It is at your peril," he cried, "if you refuse.
The meeting is impatient.   The country is in motion.   Night is approaching ; and your answer is
expected."

"Ten thousand men will rise upon the troops,
be the consequence what it may," urged a member
of the Council.

Adams trembled with the intensity of his feeling.
Hutchinson turned ashy pale, and trembled with
his fears.   He hesitated.   He feared his king ; he
feared the insulted majesty of a mighty people.
His king was afar off; the people glared upon him
where he sat.   He yielded; Colonel Dalrymple
pledged his honor to withdraw the troops, and the
first great triumph in the long war for liberty was
gained.

The following Thursday was a day of woe.   Soon
after daylight the surrounding country was astir ;
innumerable people streamed into the town by
every road.   The inhabitants were in the streets ;
the shops were closed ; all business was laid aside.
After noon the bells began to toll their mournful
tones.   For miles around the town the solemn
music fell from every steeple.   Between the hours
of four and five the funeral procession began to
move.   Caldwell and Attucks were strangers, they
were therefore buried from Faneuil Hall.   Gray's

body was taken from his brother's house. Young Maverick was brought from the desolated home of his heart-broken mother. The hearses met in King Street, near the fatal spot, thence they moved to the graves.

It was the most imposing scene ever witnessed in Boston. So numerous were the mourners that they followed the dead in ranks of six deep. Behind them stretched a long train of carriages bearing the principal people of the town.

The pageant moved through the main street to the middle burying-ground, where the four murdered bodies were laid in one grave.

5*

THE SON OF STARK.

IT was the 16th of June, 1775. The dew yet stood on the motionless grass, and the birds were in the ecstasy of their morning song, when a boy dashed furiously into the New Hampshire forest and reined in his panting horse for a rest beneath the shade. The lad was one who would attract a stranger's eye. But fifteen years of age, he was yet tall, erect, sinewy, with a bold, high forehead, and eyes of brilliant blue, sharp, and deeply set. Face and frame showed great power of body and mind. Any one who knew the famous John Stark would instantly recognize the boy as his son. Any one, too, who could have known the secret of the lad's present errand, of his strange appearance at this moment, who could have fathomed his tumultuous heart, would have seen the spirit of the sire at work in the son's young soul.

Caleb Stark was born under his grandfather's roof, when his noble father was in the far north storming the walls of Louisburg. Under the same roof he had lived, growing in stature and manli-

54

ness, and without ever a murmur of discontent, until the story of Lexington came through the forest and stirred wildly the pulses of every true heart. Then the boy grew suddenly restless, often handled his rifle, and showed a growing dislike of the quiet life on the farm. His peace of mind was gone.

The stirring news kept coming from the southward, and one day it was said that Captain John Stark had raised a regiment of men and marched to Boston, for there was going to be a great fight. The father's act met a quick response in the boy's heart. Caleb pleaded with his grandsire for leave to join the new army, but the good old man refused his consent; the camp, he said, was no place for one so young. The lad went to bed that night as usual, but only to watch sleeplessly for the still hours. Then he rose, packed all his clothing into a bag, took his rifle, crept out of the house, saddled the fleetest horse, and when the sun rose red and glaring he was far on his way to the camp. He had ridden unmercifully, from fear of pursuit, and now he was glad to give his horse a breathing-space in the cool forest.

Horse and rider were soon once more in motion, and, as the lad placed mile after mile between the old home and himself, his heart grew light and his peace of mind came back. He felt himself already a soldier. In the afternoon he fell in with a noble-looking stranger, well mounted, and wearing the uniform of a British officer.

"What is your name, my lad, and where are you going?" asked the stranger, kindly.

"I am the son of John Stark," was the proud reply, "and I'm going to join my father's regiment at Boston."

"Then you are the son of my old comrade," said the officer. "Your father and I fought five years together in the old French war. I am Major Rogers, and will gladly keep you company, as I am going the same way."

But the British major did not tell the boy the object of his mission, for he was bearing glowing offers to John Stark, hoping to win him to the king's cause. The five years' acquaintance had failed to teach him the worth of the patriot's heart.

Towards evening Caleb reached his father's camp at Medford, a few miles from Boston. He hastened to headquarters and entered unabashed. Colonel Stark looked at the boy in astonishment.

"Well, my son, what are you here for? You should have stayed at home, sir!"

"Father,"—and the lad drew himself up to full height,—"I can handle a gun as well as any one, and I've come to be a volunteer."

The father knew the spirit he was dealing with; he wasted no words.

"Very well." And he turned to George Reid,

one of his captains: "Take him to your quarters; to-morrow may be a busy day."

So Caleb Stark became a soldier.

While the young lad was sleeping his first soldier's slumber, twelve hundred men left the camp and marched, in darkness and the deepest silence, to fortify Breed's Hill. Through all the night they worked with pick and shovel, while the stars burned brightly in a cloudless sky, and up from the river came now and then the "All's well" of the sentries on the British frigates. When the stars grew dim the "All's well" suddenly ceased. Then out of the appalling stillness burst the roar of cannon and the shriek of shells; the enemy had discovered the redoubt, the immortal day's work had begun.

That morning our lad had a soldier's waking. Across the marshes came the boom of heavy guns, while the camp was alive with the shouts of officers and the rush of excited men. Soon after sunrise an officer dashed into the village, delivered an order to Colonel Stark, and spurred furiously back to Cambridge. Then the drums beat, the clamor ceased for a moment, and two hundred soldiers marched off toward the sound of the cannon.

Young Caleb began to think it would be a "busy day" indeed. His blood was aroused, and he was impatient to enter the conflict. But all the long forenoon he waited and chafed, while the cannon still roared and the tumult in the camp grew louder

c*

as fresh troops poured in from the country. About
twelve o'clock the cannonade became terrific. It
was then that the British army crossed from Boston
in barges, to drive the Americans from their intrenchments. The war-vessels redoubled their
fire and swept the lowlands with a storm of shot
and shell. Under cover of this iron tempest the
British troops landed at Moulton's Point.

While the soldiers in Stark's camp were excited
by wonder and impatience, there came across the
fields from Cambridge the clanging of bells and
the long roll of the drums. Then the roll grew
nearer and louder; it ran from camp to camp till
the deafening rattle surrounded our lad and made
his nerves tingle to the fingers' ends. Then the
fifes blew shrill and piercing, loud shouts flew back
and forth, the men formed in hot haste, and Caleb
found himself on the march. At the head of the
column, full in the boy's sight, strode the majestic
form of his father. On pressed these brave New
Hampshire men, while the roar of the cannon
grew louder. They reached the Charlestown Neck,
and the enemy's fleet came in sight. Over the
river hung dense clouds of smoke, while vivid
sheets of flame flew back and forth along the vessels' sides. The shot shrieked across the narrow
neck of land, but the troops' path lay through the
fire, and still the colonel strode on. He was asked
to quicken the pace through this galling storm.

" No !" said the cool soldier; " one fresh man in action is worth ten tired ones," and tramped steadily forward.

The troops passed over the Neck and entered the fields at the foot of Bunker Hill. Here was a long rail-fence, and Colonel Stark, making a short speech to his men, ordered breastworks to be made to keep the enemy from flanking. The men fell to work eagerly. The rails from another fence were torn up and used to strengthen the first, while the newly-mown hay in the field was piled against the frail support, and served as bulwarks for our troops.

It was now nearly three o'clock. In the redoubt on the top of the hill the patriots were quietly watching the passage of British troops across the river. As the barges drew near, our lad's comrades stopped also to gaze, for it was a sight of brilliant magnificence, a sight to fill the heart with awe. The sun blazed from a cloudless sky; the light seemed to quiver in the air. From moment to moment long lines of flame leaped from the belching ships, and through the smoke and roar the enemy's barges came on with measured stroke, blazing with scarlet uniforms and the glare of burnished brass and steel. When the troops had landed, there were over three thousand British soldiers arrayed against the defenses at Bunker Hill.

The royal artillery now opened a furious discharge, and the enemy advanced up the hill in two solid columns. Caleb stood with his comrades behind the breastworks of hay, impatiently waiting the order to fire. At this moment his heart sprang to his throat. His father leaped over the fence, advanced alone forty yards toward the enemy and drove a stake into the ground! Then he turned coolly back to his regiment. "Boys," he shouted, "the red-coats are coming up the hill. If one of you fires a gun till they reach that stake, I'll shoot him!"

On marched the British in splendid order, as if on parade. General Howe led the attack upon the rail-fence, and behind him came the Welsh fusileers, the heroes of the battle of Minden, the finest light infantry in the British army. Every nerve behind that breastwork was strained to the utmost. Our lad watched the approaching troops and waited for his father's voice. Suddenly it rang out through the deep stillness,—

"Fire!"

The New Hampshire men poured a terrible volley into the dense ranks of the enemy. The British fell by scores ; so fearful was the carnage that the proud column broke and retreated. Loud cheers went up from the regiment, and some of the men leaped over the fence to pursue the flying troops ; but Colonel Stark fiercely ordered them back. In a few moments the enemy had rallied and were advancing again to the assault, the noble form of Howe still at their head. As they drew near, under cover of a hot fire from their artillery, they discharged their muskets by ranks; but our men behind the fence held their fire. At the top of the hill the roar of musketry had again begun. Still the New Hampshire boys were quiet.

Far off to the right a terrible scene rose into the still calm air. Great columns of smoke lifted up their black heads and floated slowly away over the river. Charlestown was burning!

But our lad and his comrades had no time to gaze at this ruin. With eyes fixed keenly on the advancing troops now stepping over the dead bodies on the field, they once more waited the order to fire. At length the British were within five rods, and the command flew down the line. The havoc was horrible! Whole ranks of officers and men went down before the outburst of death; but the brave red-coats closed up and still marched steadily toward the breastwork. Volley after volley poured into them, till at one time the gallant British general was standing alone. His aids were killed; every man near him had fallen. The king's troops began to waver. The officers begged and threatened; they struck the men with their swords, and even pricked them on to the charge. Their efforts were vain. Once more the royal ranks broke and fled.

The wildest excitement now raged in the Amer ican defenses. The might of England's glory, the flower of England's army, had been twice beaten and hurled back by the "farmers and shop-boys" they so deeply despised. The most of the patriots were raw recruits, who had never before witnessed a battle. These had now lost all their natural fear and were inspired with the highest courage. But amid this little band of fifteen hundred men were many old soldiers who had fought through the French war, stormed the walls of Louisburg, and scaled the Heights of Abraham. These, by their coolness and intrepidity, acted both as check and spur to the untrained militia, and bound the whole mass into a body of sturdy and fiery soldiers whom no army could have conquered but for the sad fact which now stared them in the face.

Prescott was stalking along the parapet cheering his men to meet another assault, rejoicing in their gallant shout, "We are ready for the red-coats again!" when word was brought him that the powder was gone. But a few artillery cartridges were left; these were opened and the precious kernels distributed among the men. It was evident that the coming struggle must be hand-to-hand; and but few of the men had bayonets. These were posted at the points most likely to be scaled, and the gallant patriots waited in silence.

Meanwhile, a British reinforcement of four hundred marines had crossed the river, and General Clinton, in a light boat, was flying to aid the royal troops by his presence.

Our lad's comrades at the rail-fence had been strengthened by fresh companies from Cambridge, and were eager for the coming conflict.

Along the river, at the foot of the hill, the king's troops were marshaled, disheartened and reluctant. Many officers remonstrated against leading them again to the assault, and declared it to be down-right butchery. But Howe was enraged at his repulse; British honor was at stake; and the order was given to advance.

For a moment there was a death-like stillness as the splendid array of British soldiers stepped firmly on. Then the royal artillery dashed round the hill, took a station not far from the rail-fence, and poured a terrible fire along the whole line of the breastwork. The defenders of this post were soon driven into the redoubt, and the whole weight of the British army was hurled upon the rail-fence and the little fort. On rushed the enemy, but no shot greeted their approach. They were within twenty yards of the defenses when the Americans discharged their guns all along the line. Again the destruction was fearful. For a moment the columns wavered; but the gallant fellows had sworn this time to "conquer or die," and they sprang forward with redoubled fury. The patriot fire grew feeble for lack of powder. With a wild shout the regulars leaped upon the parapet, and the whole front rank dropped dead. Still they pressed on; by thousands they poured over the low walls and rushed upon the little band with gleaming bayonets. Then Prescott gave the order to retreat.

At the rail-fence our lad had been under a fearful fire, and was now fighting with the desperation of an old soldier. Through all the deafening roar of artillery, the death-dealing rattle of musketry, the shrieks of balls, the yells of the charging troops, and the cries of the dying, he showed a coolness and sturdiness of courage that nerved many an older patriot, and drew the highest praise from the veterans of the French war who fought by his side. During the thickest of the battle a man fell beside him pierced by a ball.

"The colonel's son is killed!" cried his comrades. A dozen men rushed to the commander, where he stood cheering on his troops to desperation.

"Sir, your son has fallen fighting!"

"If he has," roared the old lion, "it is no time to talk of private matters while the enemy are advancing in front. Back to your posts!"

Now out of the cloud of dust on the hill-top came the overpowered patriots, some flying in confusion, the most retreating in good order. Colonel

Stark saw the day was lost. At the same time he saw the desperate work his own wearied men must now do, and nobly did they respond to his appeal. The enemy's columns hurled themselves fiercely against the New Hampshire line to cut off the retreat from the fort. There followed a hand-to-hand struggle of fearful fury, till Stark, seeing his object gained, ordered a retreat, which was made with great coolness. They crossed again the narrow Charlestown Neck under a galling fire from the British ships. That night our lad worked on the intrenchments at Winter Hill, and pondered, in darkness and silence, the events of the " busy day."

Caleb Stark's sudden plunge into a soldier's life had been through a terrible ordeal, and under the test he had displayed such decision, self-reliance, coolness, and intrepidity as to give rich promise of the brilliant career which covered him with glory and honor. Meanwhile, the succeeding months were spent in eagerly learning the art of war, and in some of the most delightful social intercourse of his life.

As a cadet in Captain Reid's company his days were occupied with new duties and studies; while as son of the commander his evenings were passed in society at headquarters.

After the victorious defeat at Bunker Hill the New Hampshire regiment lay encamped behind

the Winter Hill trenches. On this beautiful spot
stood many elegant mansions, whose owners, being
loyalists, had fled into Boston. In one of these
houses Colonel Stark established his quarters. The
owner had vanished, but Madame Royal still remained at home with her family of beautiful and
charming daughters. Rejoiced at the protection
which the presence of the commander insured to
them, these accomplished ladies did all in their
power to make pleasant the stay of the American
officers. Here Caleb had his first introduction to
cultured society. Reared in the wild, unsettled
New Hampshire country, the sudden change to
the elegance and refinement of his present sur-
roundings made deep and lasting impressions on
his mind and manners. Through all his long life
he looked gratefully back to the influence of these
lovely women in the days of his youth.

But sterner faces and harsher scenes were rising
before him. Just after his sixteenth birthday, in
the opening of 1776, the boy was made an ensign
in the First New Hampshire Regiment and ordered
to New York. In the spring he went with General
Sullivan to Canada, and did noble service through
that hard campaign. On the retreat before the
British forces, the smallpox broke out among the
patriots and made savage havoc among the disheartened troops. In July, while encamped at
Chimney Point, the adjutant of Caleb's regiment

fell before the disease, and the boy was at once given the vacant post, with the rank of lieutenant. This was a situation of great responsibility, for the troops were yet raw, and upon the adjutant depends, to a large degree, the discipline of the regiment. But Caleb was as good at discipline as at fighting, and to this boy's energy and ability was due much of the splendid work done by the New Hampshire men in the battles of Princeton and Trenton,—where the lad was in the thickest of the fight.

The next spring found the seventeen-year-old adjutant at Ticonderoga. General Arthur St. Clair was in command of the fort; the garrison of two thousand men was ill-equipped, short of ammunition and provisions, and in bad humor. The duties of the boy-adjutant were therefore difficult and unpleasant, but he worked with great tact and tireless energy to make the best of the bad situation. On the 2d of July, General Burgoyne appeared before Ticonderoga with a splendid army of more than seven thousand men. St. Clair hoped for an immediate attack, for his defenses were strong, while he was unprepared to stand a siege; but three days passed by and no attempt was made by the British. Near the fort rose two lofty hills, Mount Hope and Mount Defiance, which St. Clair had strangely neglected to secure. The King's troops worked desperately through all the night of July 4th to occupy these heights. Between nightfall and dawn they cut a road through the forest, dragged up their heavy artillery, and crowned the summit with a battery.

At daybreak on the 5th of July young Adjutant Stark was wakened by the drums beating to quarters. The unusual summons brought him to his feet at once. He grasped his side-arms and rushed out, expecting to find the enemy at the walls.

What a mortifying sight filled his eyes! There, through the glimmering dawn, rose Mount Defiance, crowned with the glowing scarlet of innumerable uniforms and black with threatening cannon! The wildest excitement filled the fort. The troops expected every moment to hear the British guns open their death-dealing lips. Every man felt doomed. There seemed to be no way of escape. From their lofty position the enemy could see the slightest movement in the fort. At one glance St. Clair took in his desperate situation. There, in the early morning, he called a council of war, and young Stark was one of that band of anxious and downcast officers who now debated the best way to move.

The discussion was short. The garrison was not sufficient to defend half the works; there was no prospect of reinforcement; the enemy had cut off all supplies; their guns held perfect command of the fort; and in less than twenty-four hours the little band of patriots would be entirely surrounded. It was decided to evacuate the fort that night. No preparations could be made during the day, for the British troops could see every movement.

As soon as night dropped her friendly mantle, the Americans set rapidly to work. Every light in the fort was first extinguished. Then a furious cannonade was opened upon the British, to deceive them till the retreat should begin. Such cannon and stores as could be moved were loaded upon bateaux to cross the lake. The heavy cannon were spiked. Each man took provisions for several days and as much ammunition as he could, and at three o'clock in the morning the troops left the fort.

It was a moonlit night, but the enemy were so far away that the Americans hoped to escape unseen. In deepest silence they crossed the bridge to the fort on Mount Independence. Here the garrison joined in the retreat, and all would have gone well with the flying patriots had not General De Fermoy set fire to his quarters in the second fort as he withdrew. The building blazed high into the air, lit up the whole scene, and revealed the flight to the exultant enemy. The British general, Frazer, at once led his brigade in hot pursuit, General Reidesel and Colonel Breyman followed with their Germans and Hessians, and the Americans were thrown into terrible confusion.

In their haste and fear they threw away their arms and trampled one another to death.

Our young soldier had lost his horse at the commencement of the retreat, and was forced to struggle on foot among the panic-stricken privates. He did not think so much of the difficulties or dangers of his situation as of the disgrace of the retreat,—the bitter sting of flying before an enemy. Could he only have looked ahead but a few short weeks his chafed spirit would have been wonderfully soothed and almost reconciled. Of the three high officers who were leading this triumphant pursuit, Colonel Breyman was soon to be conquered by the lad's father on the glorious field of Bennington, while in the coming battle of Saratoga the boy was to see the gallant Frazer fall before his eyes, and to take the captive hand of Reidesel in the tent of *Brigadier-General* John Stark. But no such glorious visions now rose before the adjutant's mind. Stumbling along, bruised, despondent, out of humor, he saw just after sunrise his lost horse some way ahead, ridden by an officer. Hurrying on, young Stark overtook the beast, and discovered the rider to be the Polish general, Kosciusko. The boy angrily demanded his horse, and Kosciusko flatly refused. He had found the horse loose, he said, and he would not give him up. Caleb's spirit was at once aroused, and he did not scruple to accuse his superior of meanly stealing the beast. The great Pole roared out a reply of bitter and insulting words. The adjutant immediately demanded satisfaction, or he would force the general to combat.

"A subaltern," answered Kosciusko, "is not of sufficient rank to meet a brigadier-general."

At this moment the boy's colonel came up, on foot.

"If he is not," said that officer, "I am. This is my adjutant, general; the horse is his, and he must have him."

"Ah, Colonel Cilley," cried Kosciusko, grown suddenly polite, "if that is the case I will give up the horse."

So the boy mounted, and hoped he was free from the trampling throng; but in less than half an hour his colonel begged for a ride, and the adjutant took once more to his feet.

After this terrible night and the disastrous battle of Hubbardton, young Adjutant Stark was on duty at the headquarters of General Gates, who held command of the Northern department. One day the general called the boy in,—he had just heard of Stark's victory at Bennington.

"I am glad to see you, my boy," said General Gates, extending his hand. "Your father has opened the way for us nobly; in less than two months we shall capture Burgoyne's army. Wouldn't you like to see your father?"

The lad's heart leaped at the word, for he longed to meet his noble sire; but he was a soldier as well as a son, and discreetly answered,—

"If my regimental duties will permit, I should be very glad to visit him."

"I will find an officer to perform your duties," said the general, "and you may lead a party to Bennington and take a message to your father. I want the cannon he has taken, for I expect soon to have a brush with Burgoyne."

So the happy son set out with a mounted squad, living on the fat of the land as they went, for the Tories fled before them in every direction, leaving their stock in their barns, and even their food on the tables.

But Caleb's visit was short; his general had said he was expecting "a brush with Burgoyne," and the lad's heart was restless to be back before the fight. In a few days he was flying over the roads to Saratoga, and reached his regiment just in time for the battle.

The 19th of September began calm and cloudless; there was a Sabbath stillness in the air. The hills around the village of Stillwater were covered with frost, and at their feet lay the Hudson, gleaming in the sun. It was not this peaceful beauty, however, that filled the boy's eyes as he stood in the door of his tent and looked abroad.

Thousands of white tents covered the lowlands

by the river, and glimmered through the woods upon the hills. Through the keen frosty air came the beat of drums from the British camp, and soon the gleam of bayonets and the glow of scarlet uniforms shone bright amid the peaceful green of the forest. The army of Burgoyne was forming in line of battle. Toward noon the British slowly advanced, in three divisions.

Our young adjutant was the first in the fight. Under the command of Arnold he moved forward with part of his regiment, and with Morgan's riflemen rushed upon the Canadian and Indian troops on the hills and drove them in every direction. So fierce was this charge that the men dashed through and past the enemy's ranks before they could check their speed.

A British force under Major Forbes then fell impetuously upon the patriots and scattered them in the woods; but only for a moment. While our adjutant was rallying his men, the loud, clear whistle of Morgan pierced the forest; then the wood trembled to the wild cheers of his followers, who had lost sight of their idol among the dense trees, and now flocked to the ringing sound.

On they leaped to the charge, our gallant boy standing in his stirrups, and wielding his sword with fury. For a few moments the conflict was fierce, but the opponents were equally matched and both parties finally retired.

The battle thus opened was now raging all along the line. With the left wing under Arnold our young officer advanced rapidly, to cut off Frazer's division and turn the British flank. Struggling on through the dense forest, the patriots suddenly met the troops of Frazer face to face. The fiery Arnold was the first to recover from the surprise. With voice like a trumpet he rang out the order to charge; the men sprang like tigers upon the foe; 'mid the thickest of the tumult were the flashes of the brave boy's sword. The enemy were overwhelming in numbers; hand-to-hand the conflict raged for an hour; the desperate courage of the patriots was grasping complete victory, when the British were joined by fresh troops and artillery, and our baffled heroes fell back.

Far into the night the battle lived, when the exhausted armies withdrew and lay upon their arms till morning. Young Adjutant Stark had been conspicuous through all the day. For ten long hours he had been in the saddle, fighting with the desperation of a madman; few as were his years, he had shown a dashing bravery, an unconquerable endurance, of which any veteran might be proud. Now he flung himself upon his blankets to gather breath and strength for the morrow.

But the morrow was a quiet day. The dull, cloudy morning found the British in possession of the battle-field, but disinclined to try the battle again. The patriots strengthened their intrench-ments, while Burgoyne fell back to his old camp.

The next two weeks were spent by both armies in preparing for the final contest. Our boy-adju-tant was upon his feet night and day. The ravages of battle were evident in his regiment. The troops were re-organized; raw recruits came in,—and the severest burdens and responsibility rested on the lad's young shoulders. His regiment must be brought into perfect fighting trim, and he must do it. The noble services of the New Hampshire men in the next great battle showed how gloriously the boy performed his work.

Burgoyne was in despair at not receiving re-inforcements from New York; his supplies were completely cut off by the vigilant patriots; his army was on short allowance. He was now forced to fight or retreat. His proud heart could not con-sent to fly before the men he had publicly scorned, and he resolved upon a final struggle.

Early on the 7th of October, Burgoyne moved forward at the head of his choicest troops to within three-fourths of a mile of the American camp. Just before his advance began, General Gates had sent out a detachment to flank the British and at-tack their outposts, but the order was recalled as soon as Burgoyne's movement was discovered. In a short time firing was heard in the woods, and the American pickets fell back before an attacking party of Canadians, Indians, and Tories.

Our young adjutant was now in a condition of very natural anxiety. As soon as the firing was heard his soldierly instinct assured him that a desperate day had opened. He knew that the fate of Burgoyne hung upon this rising sun. The struggle would be terrible; would the First New Hampshire —raw recruits and all—do its duty? This was an absorbing question to the young officer. He felt himself greatly responsible for the conduct of his regiment; but while he dashed about hither and thither to see that his men were ready for action, the fire in the woods grew sharper, came nearer, when the stentorian voice of Morgan ordered a charge, and the fiery test of the boy's work began.

Again the lad was the first in action. He rushed on with the riflemen of Morgan. The onslaught was so fierce that the British broke and fled in confusion. They were chased close up to the enemy's lines, when the pursuers, finding the royal troops drawn out in battle array, retired in triumph to their camp.

An hour was now spent by the two armies in securing their positions, in marching and countermarching, in endeavors to outgeneral one another. The British grenadiers under the noble Major Ackland rested on a hill which stood behind Mill Creek. These gallant soldiers formed the left wing of the royal troops. Its centre consisted of British and Germans, under Phillips and Reidesel, while the right wing was composed of the light infantry, led by Earl Balcarras. In advance of the right wing, General Frazer commanded five hundred picked men, waiting to assault the American flank as soon as the battle should begin.

General Gates now sent forward a corps to drive Frazer from his position, and at the same moment ordered an attack upon the British left.

It was now about half-past two. Against the British left wing our troops advanced, and foremost among them was Colonel Cilley's First New Hampshire Regiment, with our lad marching beside his commander. In profound silence they moved steadily up the hill, whose summit was covered with the British grenadiers and the British artillery. Our men were ordered not to fire until after the first discharge from the enemy's batteries. On they moved, amid an appalling silence. Suddenly a terrific rattle and roar burst from the crown of the hill. A storm of bullets and grape-shot swept down the slope, but mainly passed over the advancing troops and tore through the trees overhead. Then with loud yells the patriots rushed forward, firing rapidly by ranks. They dashed up to the cannons' mouths; the assault was furious, but the British were brave and stubborn. Then began one of the fiercest struggles of the whole

war. Our lad was with his colonel, at the head of
his troops, at the death-dealing mouths of the British cannon. Back and forth the contending forces
surged like the tides of the sea. Around one of
the cannon the fight was the hottest. Here stood
Colonel Cilley,—here were the young adjutant and
his brave followers. All his fears for the men's behavior were fled; the noble fellows charged the
cannon, and captured it; the British rushed forward and took it back; then our lad led another
assault, and once more the death-filled brass piece
was held by the patriots. Five times was this cannon captured and recaptured. At the last charge,
Colonel Cilley leaped upon the gun, waved his
sword over his head, consecrated the cannon to
the cause of liberty, wheeled its muzzle against the
enemy, and poured their own shot into their doomed
ranks. The victors' shouts rose above the roar of
the battle; they rushed again upon the grenadiers,
and drove them from the field. In this charge the
young adjutant received a shot in his left arm.
Almost stunned by the wound, yet rejoicing that
his sword-arm was safe, he rushed on at the head
of his triumphant troops.

Major Ackland fell, shot through both legs, and
was sent back to the American camp. Disheartened at the fall of their leader and the fearful
slaughter among their own ranks, the British did
not return to the combat.

From now until evening the battle raged with terrific fury. Our lad fought through all that afternoon, until, just at sunset, knowing well that the victory was surely ours, he was forced to leave the field, overcome with loss of blood and with exhaustion. But the battle was over.

Just as the sun rested a moment on the tree-tops for its plunge into darkness, the roar of the American artillery suddenly ceased; then a heavy boom broke the air and echoed from hill to hill; another and another followed from the same gun.

Gates had just learned that the troops he had been cannonading were marching in funeral procession to bury the noble General Frazer, who fell at the head of his men. The soldier's heart was touched. The cannonading was stopped, and in its stead the minute-gun poured forth its heavy notes of mourning for the gallant dead.

Night now fell softly between the contending armies, bearing peace on its wings. The frightful roar of artillery, the yells of charging columns, gave place to the shrieks of the wounded, the groans of the dying.

Ten days passed on, and the young adjutant witnessed the grand pageant of Burgoyne's surrender. In the quarters of his father and of General Gates the lad met the conquered generals, and listened to the long conversation between his father and Burgoyne on the subject of the old French war.

The adjutant's wound was severe, and unfitted him for present service. Still he clung to his sword and would not retire from the army. In a few weeks his father, who had become a brigadier-general, appointed the lad his brigade-major, and at the age of eighteen Caleb Stark was aide-de-camp, brigade-major, and adjutant-general of the Northern department.

THE YOUNG WEST INDIAN.

It was the 6th of July, 1774. A vast concourse of people thronged " The Fields," or what is now the City Hall Park, in the city of New York. From the faces of the great multitude one could learn somewhat of the varied and contending emotions which brought them hither. Here could be seen both wild excitement and cool, calm determination; the eagerness of hope and the hesitancy of fear.

This was, indeed, no ordinary meeting. While it assembled the great heart of the city well-nigh ceased to throb; the streets grew quiet; a shadow fell upon many faces, and more glowed with a deep, strong light, while the shadow and the glow told plainly to the watcher who was Tory and who was Patriot.

Boston was prostrate under the foot of tyranny; her harbor was closed by British ships, and her inhabitants suffering destitution. This cruel indignity had aroused all the American colonies. The long stretch of Atlantic seaboard spoke as

with one voice and gave as with one hand. The
sea was lively with white sails that had been raised
in Southern ports to bear generous gifts to suffering Boston; while from the depths of the primeval
forest beyond the far Alleghanies came the loving
tribute of the hardy pioneers who made their
harvest with the rifle and the spade. With con-
tributions of rice, wheat, flour, and cattle came
also ringing words of cheer and encouragement.
The great colony of New York proposed a congress of deputies to discuss the situation of Boston,
and to take measures for securing the common
rights. Earnest opposition was made to this startling proposal, and now the patriots had called this
meeting in " The Fields" to take some action that
should be decisive.

On the outskirts of the vast throng men formed
in little groups, unable to hear the speakers, and
discussed in earnest tones the topics that filled
every mind. Beyond the outer verge, in the
shadow of some noble trees, a slight, frail lad,
a few months past his seventeenth birthday, paced
thoughtfully to and fro, talking to himself in
deep, full under-tones of voice. Attracted by the
boy's appearance, some men drew near, and led
him into conversation. The strength and clearness of his thoughts, the soundness of his views,
impressed his listeners with admiration. They
marveled to find such power in one so young.

They urged him to go forward and address the meeting, but he shrank from such boldness. He was but a boy, and he was unknown; his words would have no weight. Yet his soul was in a glow, filled with the mighty problems the throng had met to settle; he entered the dense crowd and listened with the keenest attention to the successive speakers.

As one and another addressed the multitude, and yet many points were left untouched, the boy's face began to shine with an eager light. His head was bent forward; he grew restless; at last, unable to restrain himself longer, he pressed through the mass and reached the platform.

As he stepped out into sight, a myriad eyes were turned upon him in wonder; a deep silence fell upon the vast throng.

The lad drew his slender form to its full height, and looked down into those eager, wondering eyes. For a moment his situation seemed appalling; he trembled. He opened his mouth to speak. The words came slowly: his tongue faltered. But there glowed beneath that boyish form a soul more powerful than the concentrated energy of the thousands who now waited for its utterance. They had not long to wait. In a few moments every trace of timidity was gone. With clear, ringing voice he set the grand theme of liberty before them in new and enchanting light. He gathered the hanging threads of the previous speeches and wove them, with wonderful art, into a robe of glory for the new goddess of freedom. He poured forth a torrent of resistless logic and passionate eloquence, until every heart thrilled like harp-strings in the hand of a player. His slight form seemed to grow gigantic. Every eye in the vast throng flashed fire. His burning eyes caught the flashes and hurled them back in a blaze of light. Every muscle, every fibre of his impassioned body was eloquent; he seemed to speak with a thousand tongues. And when, at last, he demanded unyielding resistance to tyranny, described the means of success, and showed " the waves of rebellion sparkling with fire and washing back on the shores of England the wrecks of her power, of her wealth, and of her glory," the breathless multitude burst into a wild tumult of applause:

" It is a collegian! it is a collegian!"

This young stranger was Alexander Hamilton. The best blood of Scotland and of Huguenot France met in his veins when, on the 11th of January, 1757, he came to life on the island of Nevis, in the Antilles. His birthplace was a paradise, but it could not long hold the restless mind of the ambitious youth. At the merchant's desk, where he was placed at twelve years of age, his thoughts stretched out afar, beyond the narrow boundaries of the little isle, and built a hope of great deeds

and well-earned glory. To a young schoolmate
he wrote, at this early period, "I contemn the
groveling condition of a clerk, and would willingly
risk my life, though not my character, to exalt my
station."

At thirteen he was placed at the head of the
establishment!

In 1772 a fearful hurricane swept the Leeward
Islands with destruction and death. A vivid account of the calamity, which appeared in a newspaper of a neighboring island, was traced to young
Hamilton. His talent was immediately recognized,
and it was determined to give him a thorough edu-
cation.

He was sent to New York. On the passage
the vessel took fire, and was saved with the utmost
difficulty.

After a short season of preparation at a school
in Elizabethtown, New Jersey, the boy entered
King's College, now Columbia College, in New
York, as a private student, choosing his own
course of study. He at once displayed remarkable powers of writing and debate. He composed
graceful verses, and one of his hymns, of much
feeling, is preserved to this day.

Ere he was yet conscious of it he was drawn
into the approaching struggle. The friends of the
royal cause filled the New York papers with fierce
denunciations of the hopes and feelings of the

8

patriots. The brilliant young student burlesqued
these tirades with the most biting satires.

The stranger-boy watched the rapid course of
events with a keen and thoughtful mind. His sympathies were strongly aroused, while at the same
time he saw opening before him a path of distinc-
tion and glory. He pondered the issue in all its
bearings, and threw himself into the patriot cause
with body and soul.

Thus snatched from obscurity by a noble ambition, covered by the hand of God from the terrible
tornado, rescued from the fierce fire and the savage
sea, Alexander Hamilton had appeared to the astonished throng on this great 6th of July like a
being from another sphere.

" The Young West Indian," as he was called by
his comrades, had suddenly begun his brilliant
course.

He soon entered the lists in deadly earnest as
a champion of liberty. For some time he concealed his authorship, and we might never have
known whose powerful mind and fearless hand
were dealing such noble blows for the rights of
America had not his college room-mate told the
story.

In rapid and startling succession young Hamilton launched newspaper articles and pamphlets
against the astonished champions of tyranny. He
first defended boldly the destruction of tea in

Boston. He then attacked fiercely the cruel and insane policy of the British government. Soon there appeared two pamphlets of great power and artfulness, signed "A Westchester Farmer," and written by an Episcopal clergyman named Seabury, a learned man and stanch loyalist. His arguments were wily and strong, calculated to affect the wavering, of whom there were many in both parties. The timid among the patriots were disconcerted by the "Farmer's" boastful words, but the great mass of faithful souls were highly enraged. At one place, during a county meeting, the two pamphlets were dressed in a coat of tar and feathers, and nailed to the pillory.

A more effective answer soon appeared. The brilliant college-boy came forward as the David who should slay this dreaded Goliath. Under the name of "A Sincere Friend to America" he attacked the clergyman's arguments with subtle reasoning and impetuous force. Fulfilling the promise of his title, he exposed his sophistry, detected his artifices, and ridiculed his wit. Then, with a bold daring, he coolly discussed the advantages of taking arms in open rebellion, and even pointed out the mode of warfare best calculated to win success. At last he eloquently exhorted his readers to maintain, at any cost, "the sacred rights of mankind, which are written," he said, "as with a sunbeam, in the whole volume of human nature, by the hand of the Divinity itself, and can never be erased or obscured by mortal power."

Deep arguments, startling courage, noble words, for a boy of seventeen! So remarkable, indeed, that not one of the thousands who were dazzled, cheered, encouraged, had the slightest suspicion of their true source. Only his room-mate was in the secret, and to him the productions were shown before they were sent to the press.

Into the enemy's camp these writings fell like bomb-shells. To the friends of liberty they were as the ringing trumpet-blast before the victory. But both friends and enemies united in one cry, " Who is it? Who is the author?"

They were charged to the greatest minds in the patriot party, and when finally it was said that a college student was the author, many would not believe it, and those who did believe were lost in wonder and admiration. The Tory president of the college, Dr. Cooper, laughed at the idea that such a boy could have written those powerful pages.

But the growing mass of patriots at once raised the youth to the throne of leadership. He was called " the vindicator of Congress."

" Sir," said that noble soldier, Marinus Willett, " Sears was a warm man, McDougall was strong-minded, and Jay tempered and controlled; but

Hamilton, after these great writings, became our oracle."

It is a remarkable fact that in these pamphlets the young lad was the first to predict the growth of cotton in America. "Several of the southern colonies," he wrote, "are so favorable to it, that with due cultivation, in a couple of years, they would afford enough to clothe the whole continent."

With keen, far-seeing eye, the college-boy detected the approaching inevitable war. He joined a volunteer corps under the lead of Major Fleming, a thorough soldier, who had been an adjutant in the British army. He devoted himself now to his studies and to drill. He laid a sound foundation of military knowledge, while at the same time he pursued his college course with unabated zeal. The corps was composed of young gentlemen of the city in good circumstances, who were preparing themselves to hold rank in the American army, when it should be formed. They called themselves "Hearts of Oak." Their uniform was green, and their leathern caps bore the bold motto, "Freedom or Death."

Every morning now saw the student-soldier exercising with the corps in the church-yard of St. George's chapel, in Beekman Street. He acquired the manual of arms and the rudiments of battalion-drill with astonishing celerity. He bought books

8*

on the art of war, and spent the night hours in mastering their principles.

His first active service came sooner than he expected. As matters drew near a crisis, the "Committee of One Hundred" determined to secure the cannon that defended the city. They ordered Captain Lamb, who commanded the artillery, to seize the guns at the grand battery, and take them to a place of safety. The fiery young West Indian could not be absent from such an enterprise. Great, black, British ships of war lay in the stream, with guns shotted and port-holes open, jealously watching every movement in the city. There was danger in the undertaking, which was the first active move against the enemy. It appealed to the boy's nature; he must certainly go. He collected fifteen of his fellow-students, and led them to Captain Lamb.

At nine o'clock in the evening, on the 23d of August, 1775, the little band quietly approached the battery. The dark walls frowned upon them in gloomy silence. It was a moment to fill every thoughtful mind, for this was open rebellion against the greatest power on the earth. But the patriots had counted well the cost. With unwavering steps they marched into the fort and began the dismantling. Something black was soon seen moving on the water. It drew nearer; scarlet uniforms and bright steel made light in the darkness. It was a barge from the *Asia* man-of-war, filled with armed men sent to watch the patriots. Suddenly the report of a musket pierced the stillness, and a ball whizzed viciously past the ears of the workers. They seized their muskets and poured a volley into the crowded barge. Shrieks came up from the water; the boat flew swiftly back to the ship, while the patriots sprang to their work with redoubled energy. When the barge reached the *Asia*, there were several men killed and wounded to be lifted aboard. Captain Vandeput was enraged. He ran out his cannon and sent three balls into the city in rapid succession. With the roar of the guns, young Hamilton's heart beat with furious zeal. This was what he had wanted! This was the beginning of war, indeed!

Rapidly the cannon were dismounted, one by one, and dragged into the street. Captain Lamb ordered the drums to beat to arms. In a moment the church-bells rang out their furious tones. People rushed into the streets; the whole city was in uproar. Our lad cheered on his young followers, who worked with desperation. His quick mind took in the situation; his dauntless heart rejoiced in it. Behind him were rolling drums, clanging bells, the shouts of men and the screams of frightened women. Before, in the black night, lay the great war-ship loaded with death. Suddenly a terrific roar followed a blaze of light that illumined the river. It was a broadside from the *Asia!* A man fell by the boy's side; the blood splashed his clothes, but he worked on unconcerned. Another and another broadside! The thunder reverberated from the Jersey shore! Behind, in the city, were heard the crash of buildings and the terrible tumult of the terror-stricken crowds. Thousands of men, women, and children thronged the streets, rushing into the open country for their lives. The uproar was fearful. The people trampled on one another as they staggered on beneath the loads of household goods they were unwilling to leave. But amid these dreadful scenes, in the face of death, and fears for their flying families, the little band of patriots worked steadily on, and brought off every gun from the fort,—twenty-one iron eighteen-pounders and several smaller cannon. These were hastily dragged through the city and concealed. Some of them did splendid service afterward for the cause of American freedom.

Young Hamilton, with his fifteen boy-soldiers, claimed some of the guns as trophies. Amid wild enthusiasm they hauled them to the college green. The president stormed and threatened, but the boys had faced British fire, and were not to be frightened by Tory menaces. In the teeth of the president's fury they buried two cannon under the

college trees. These were afterwards dug up, and
stood at the gateway of the college until it was
torn down in 1856.

The tumult in the city continued. The King's
store was attacked and plundered. Violent mobs
rushed from place to place. The Connecticut
troops marched to the city to protect the inhabitants. Bands of "Liberty Boys" roamed through
the streets threatening destruction to every Tory.
They rushed to King's College to seize Dr. Cooper,
the president. Young Hamilton was there. His
sense of justice was strong; he had no love for
mobs. On came the infuriated throng, howling for
vengeance. As they surged up to the building,
Hamilton sprang upon the steps. He stretched
out his arms; the "Liberty Boys" recognized the
wonderful genius who was so feared by their
enemies; they became calm. The student addressed them; he remonstrated against violence,
and showed why so noble a cause as liberty
should be served with reverence. His object
was to detain the mob until the president could
escape.

Imagine his consternation when, in the midst of
his generous speech, the frightened doctor leaned
out from an upper window, and yelled,—

"Don't listen to him, gentlemen; he's crazy!
he's crazy!"

But the terrified president escaped. He rushed

down the back stairs, flew to the water-side, and was taken off by a man-of-war.

Twice again this law-loving young rebel against tyranny threw himself in the path of raging mobs which were profaning the holy name of liberty. When " Travis's mob" was seeking the life of an innocent man who had aroused their anger, the boy checked them in their wild course and turned aside their wrath. When, in the next November, Captain Isaac Sears entered the city at the head of seventy-five light-horse, and attacked the Tory press of James Rivington, young Hamilton appealed in vain to the better sense of the galled patriots. "King Sears" had been goaded past endurance by Rivington's Gazette. He destroyed the presses, and carried off the types to melt into bullets. Hamilton then called for men to join him in pursuing the marauders and recapturing the types. But for once the people would not rally to their idolized young leader. Popular sentiment was with " King Sears."

Through all this winter the lad studied diligently the art of war, and learned gunnery from a British bombardier. Meanwhile, his future great rival in every step of life, Aaron Burr, of about the same age, was starving in the savage forests of Maine, leading the desperate night-assault on Quebec, and bearing from the scene of death the lifeless body of his general.

Early in the spring of 1776, Hamilton, now nineteen years old, spoke of revisiting the West Indies
to increase his slender funds. The New York patriots were alarmed at the prospect of losing their
idol. They begged him not to leave them, but to
remain and lead them to victory in the mighty
struggle. The lad was pleased with their devotion.

"Well, my friends," he replied, "if you are determined I shall stay with you and take part in
your just and holy cause, you must raise for me a
full company of artillery."

He was so young that some of the scarred veterans of "the old French war" shook their gray
beards and doubted his fitness. He passed a
rigorous examination, and on the 14th of March
was appointed "Captain of the provincial company
of artillery."

The young captain entered upon his duties en-
thusiastically. He immediately enlisted several
veteran artillerists, recruited his company, spent
the last money he possessed in equipping them,
and drilled them so rigorously and constantly that
they soon reached a high state of discipline.

One day, in this summer of 1776, General Greene
was crossing "The Fields," when he noticed a company of artillery drilling upon the grounds. Their
movements were quick and beautifully accurate.
His soldier's eye was captivated, and he stopped

to watch. As the company approached he saw with amazement that its leader was a mere boy,— very slight in figure too. The lad's face was striking; his commands were quick and soldierly; and his whole bearing showed great intelligence and self-reliance. The general called the boy-captain, and entered into conversation. His wonder now increased; he recognized extraordinary genius. He invited Captain Hamilton to his quarters; he took every occasion to cultivate his acquaintance, and some time afterwards introduced him to the commander-in-chief.

One of the boy's first acts in his new position of artillery-captain has had a vast influence on the armies of the whole civilized world. He at once wrote a letter to the New York Convention, recommending promotion from the ranks for efficiency and gallantry. His plan was adopted, and gradually came into use in nearly every country; Great Britain being the last to accept it, a century after its origin.

His active genius was already at work, also, on that marvelous plan of government which he afterwards so powerfully pressed upon the Continental Congress. The "pay book" of his company is a storehouse of deep thoughts on these vast themes, mixed in with his accounts with his soldiers.

Stirring events now came on with a bewildering rush. On the 9th of July General Washington caused the new Declaration of Independence to be read at the head of every brigade in the city of New York. That same evening the equestrian statue of George III. was pulled down and melted into bullets. The day before this General Howe landed nine thousand British troops on Staten Island. In a few days Admiral Howe appeared with a large fleet, followed shortly by General Clinton and Admiral Parker, who came from their disastrous attack on Charleston. By the 12th of July thirty thousand British veterans looked down from the peaceful woods of Staten Island upon the little patriot army in the city.

Washington at once threw up intrenchments on Brooklyn Heights. The young artillery-captain was wide awake. He crossed to Brooklyn and surveyed the American position with a critical eye. He became alarmed as he thought of the prospect. He hurried back to the city, and boldly wrote a letter of advice to the commander-in-chief, but signed no name. He argued strongly against risking an action between raw militia and the veteran troops of England, and warmly urged a retreat to the high grounds of the main land. The stately Washington was astonished at the writer's boldness, while he admired the genius displayed.

The line of defenses at Brooklyn was very long, and several passes were not properly guarded.

E   9

On the evening of the 26th of August General Clinton captured an important pass, and early in the morning of the 27th began the fierce battle of Long Island. When the sun sank over the field of blood, one-third of the five thousand patriots who had so gallantly contested the day were killed, wounded, or prisoners. Retreat or total destruction was Washington's alternative. In a wonderful manner the God of nations threw his protection around the little army. The morning of the 28th broke in fog. Concealed from the enemy's view, the patriots crossed over to New York. At six the next morning the hardy boatmen had landed nine thousand soldiers with baggage and munitions in the city of refuge, and yet the retreat was undiscovered by the British. The young Captain Hamilton, with his artillery, brought up the rear, being the last to leave. His baggage was in a cart, drawn by a single horse. Some of the artillery horses had been killed in the battle, and one gun was reluctantly left behind. Still the poor beasts were overtaxed, and staggered in the traces. They were urged on, but the retreat dragged. The faithful young officer took prompt action. He abandoned his personal baggage— comprising all his effects, and he was nearly penni-less—and hitched his horse to the cannon. The battery was brought off in safety.

The British now rapidly wove a skillful web

around the patriot army. After weeks of anxiety Washington withdrew from the city, and fortified himself strongly on the Heights of Harlem.

The young Captain Hamilton here found his military studies, his quick insight, and tireless activity, of great service to his adopted country. He was constantly engaged on the intrenchments, where he was looked to for aid and counsel in every emergency.

Washington brought everything under his own eye. He inspected every battalion and every earth-work. One day he noticed with unusual pleasure the skill displayed in some defenses which were rapidly assuming formidable shape. Dashing hither and thither, giving clear, rapid orders, show-ing a perfect knowledge of the work, was a boy in the uniform of a captain of artillery.

The great chief watched him a few moments with admiration and joy. He then called the lad to his side, and discovered him to be the brilliant young West Indian. He led him to his marquée, conversed with him on military matters, and dis-missed him with praise. This interview made a deep impression on Washington. The army was new, and it was difficult to get officers who under-stood their business.

This brief conversation had excited in the gen-eral a warm feeling of friendship and an admira-tion that bordered on wonder. He had discovered a remarkable genius.   From that hour the chief's eye never lost sight of Hamilton.

The plan of action before urged upon Washington, in the boy's anonymous letter, was now adopted.   It was determined to risk no general engagement, but to harass the enemy unceasingly and retreat slowly from hill to hill.   General Howe bent all his energies to force the Americans to a battle.   Toward the middle of October the enemy advanced, and Washington retreated to the hills around White Plains.   Here, intrenched upon the heights, the patriots were protected on the right flank by the river Bronx and on the left by an upland lake.   On Chatterton's Hill, half a mile southwest of the Bronx, a body of militia was stationed to further protect the right wing.

At dawn of a beautiful autumn day, the 28th of October, the British army moved forward in two columns, the right under Clinton and the left under the Hessian De Heister.   It was a glorious spectacle, but unwelcome enough to the patriot-leaders, who felt unable to cope with so powerful a force.   The British chasseurs drove in the advance-guard of the Americans, when the columns divided and the two lines of glowing scarlet and gleaming steel swept toward the village, one to the west, the other to the east.   Howe at once saw the commanding position of Chatterton's Hill, and determined to drive the Americans from their vantage-ground. The keen eye of Washington noticed this movement. Reinforcements were immediately sent to the hill, and young Captain Hamilton was ordered to choose a position for his artillery. The boy led his company to the brow of the hill, and soon his guns were disposed with a master-hand. Howe began, towards noon, to concentrate his whole force upon this important eminence. A battery opened a hot fire on the patriots, and, under cover of the rapid discharges, the Hessians moved forward. Reaching the swollen Bronx, filled with driftwood, they refused to enter the dangerous stream. They began to throw across it a temporary bridge. The young artillery-captain was ordered to check the enemy from crossing. In a moment his guns were limbered, and the horses dashed down the hill at break-neck speed. He halted behind a little grove, which would conceal him from the British fire, and planted his two field-pieces on a ledge of rocks commanding the nearly-completed bridge. Instantly he hurled a torrent of shot among the astonished Hessians. The bridge was crushed. Killed and mangled men dropped into the angry stream; the Hessians on the bank were thrown into wild confusion. The little captain was delighted with his success. He cheered his men to work furiously; charge upon charge of deadly shot was poured into the enemy. The Hessians fell back.

At this moment a brigade of British troops, under General Leslie, rushed to the rescue. They waded the river and dashed upon Hamilton's battery with fixed bayonets and appalling yells. The boy's commands rang out fierce and rapid. This was the work he had longed to see. He had studied for it, drilled for it, spent his last money for it, and his heart beat with wild joy. Every nerve and muscle was in fierce activity. The gallant Englishmen sprang up the hill in the face of his terrible fire. Again and again his guns hurled their deadly hail through the charging column, mowing a swath to the water's edge. The enemy fell back bewildered, almost destroyed. The Hessians had crossed, and now rushed to the support. They were beaten back by the desperate artillerymen. Suddenly a roll of drums and the blare of trumpets sounded above the strife. Harcourt's light dragoons came on with impetuous speed! The militia lost their presence of mind; they wavered; they fled tumultuously. Hamilton, undaunted, still stood by his guns. While fighting fiercely, an orderly brought him word to retire. In the midst of a storm of musketry he wheeled and took off his cannon without loss.

That night this wonderful boy of nineteen was the idol of the camp. The officers crowded around him and were proud to grasp his hand. His skill and bravery had saved the army; yet this was his first battle. He had laid a noble foundation for his military fame.

His impetuous daring was soon again made manifest. On the 16th of November, Fort Washington, after a terrible resistance, fell into the hands of the enemy. The possession of this fort was of the utmost importance. Young Hamilton's heart was filled with grief and rage. He hastened to the commander-in-chief and begged for permission to retake the fort by storm! But there were no men to spare for such desperate service. Sad and pleased, Washington refused his pleading; but he was fast marking the boy for his own.

Now came the gloomy retreat through the Jerseys. Hotly followed by eight thousand troops under Cornwallis, the three thousand half-clothed, poorly-equipped patriots reached New Brunswick unmolested. But just as their rear was crossing the Raritan, the British advance came in sight.

Captain Hamilton had been watching for this very calamity. He took in the high grounds by the river at a glance, dashed off with his battery, planted it on a commanding spot, and poured his fire into the advancing enemy. The pursuers were taken by surprise. Bewildered for a moment, they soon rallied and charged the guns. Once and again they were hurled back by the gallant youth.

Far off, on another height, stood the commander-in-chief, anxiously watching the passage of his little army. His pain, when he first caught sight of the pursuing enemy, was now changed to hope. Delighted by the wisdom, the quickness, and the fiery courage of the artillery officer who was thus snatching the flying army from destruction, Washington sent Colonel Fitzgerald to ask his name. When the aide returned and told his chief that it was Alexander Hamilton, the young captain was requested to present himself at headquarters at the first halt of the army.

Against fearful odds, young Hamilton held his ground hour after hour, until the patriots had reached Princeton in safety. Then he suddenly left his station and fled before the enraged enemy. He had accomplished his design; again he had saved the army.

When the company of artillery marched into Princeton, young Hamilton was the observed of all eyes. Men who watched the entry of that gallant battery have left us vivid pictures of the scene. Amid wild enthusiasm the brave fellows marched up the hill to the village. Notwithstanding their severe service and terrible exhaustion, they came on in the most perfect order. At their head was a mere boy, a slight, frail figure and beardless face. Shouts and cheers rent the air:

"It is Hamilton! it is Hamilton!"

But the lad tramped on unconcerned. He marched beside the first gun, his cocked hat pulled low down over his eyes, looking neither to the right nor to the left. One hand was resting on the cannon, and every now and then he patted it as if he loved it tenderly. And no doubt he did.

He soon went to headquarters, and was long detained. What passed there is not known; but it *is* known that after fighting his guns nobly through the battles of Trenton and Princeton, and refusing brilliant offers from several American generals, he accepted, at the age of twenty, the rank of lieutenant-colonel, and the position of aide-de-camp to the commander-in-chief.

LITTLE BURR.

The opening of September, 1775, found the American camp at Cambridge in great confusion. Officers were hurriedly going about, drawing off their chosen men from the different groups of comrades, camp-messes were broken up, and long companionship was severed; for there was need of true and hardy soldiers who could face the perils of a terrible service.

On a narrow pallet in one of the barracks a boy lay tossing with fever. When the smoke and roar of the battle of Bunker Hill rolled southward the word of alarm, this lad was at Litchfield, in Connecticut, dividing his time between the study of law and flirting with the village maidens,—the girls getting by far the largest part. His quick ear caught at once the note of war, and his quick blood eagerly responded. He threw away his books, mounted a fleet horse, and started off on the long ride to Elizabethtown, New Jersey. Here lived a bosom-friend, a lad whose name was Ogden. The two comrades made hasty preparations, and were soon flying over the road to the great camp at Cambridge. Once there, they expected to be led to battle. The British were in Boston, and thousands of eager patriots were within an hour's march of the city, burning to attack the enemy. But the hot summer days wore on, and nothing was done.

The soldiers murmured and swore, and some even then talked of treason. But there was a terrible secret which these honest, fiery hearts could not know,—the American army had no powder. How well it was for us that the hostile army over the river caught no hint of this fearful fact! The two boys had come to fight; but fighting seemed every day to get farther off than ever; and at last the young student had fretted and chafed himself into a fever.

On this day, when all was commotion in the camp, he lay upon his hard bed and heard loud voices in a neighboring room. Ogden's voice was among them, and the sick lad, intently listening, was startled by a few strange words. He called his friend. Ogden came to the bedside, and was astonished at the eager light in the fevered eyes.

" Ogden, tell me what they are talking about!"

" Well, Burr, my boy, the dashing Colonel Arnold is going to march, with a thousand men, through the wilds of Maine, to join Montgomery and take Quebec."

The sick boy sprang from his bed and began to dress.

"What are you doing?" cried Ogden, horrified, and seizing the clothes.

"I am going!" calmly replied his friend.

"Going? going where?"

"To Quebec, sir, if you must know."

"Why, Burr, you are crazy!"

"Not so crazy as you think." And feebly stretching out his wasted hand, he added,—

"Be kind enough to pass me my boots."

So, dressed and leaning on the arm of his remonstrating friend, the sick young soldier staggered out into the busy scene. Here he was stormed with exclamations and remonstrances. His high spirit and winning nature had made him friends through all the army, and now they crowded around him with hearty affection and entreaties. But young Burr had a tremendous will. He was dying to fight; now he would fight to live. No pleadings could change his purpose. Under the excitement and joy of preparation he soon threw off his sickness,—the dauntless mind brought the body back to health; and when the drums and fifes called the men to fall in on their march to Newburyport, the young law-student was in the ranks.

Of these eleven hundred gallant hearts that now beat so high, how many would have gone forth upon this terrible march through the wilderness could they have seen the appalling end? *This* one, at least, whoever might recoil. Having once put his hand to an enterprise, neither now nor ever was Aaron Burr the man to turn back, though legions of demons should meet him in the way.

The little army were not kept in the strictest order on this forty-mile march to the port of embarkation. The men tramped on in groups, for it was a friendly country, and no enemy was near. Young Burr had equipped a few men at his own expense, and as he walked along with these comrades a horseman was heard clattering over the road behind them, and, dashing up to the group, he asked for Aaron Burr. The lad stepped out. The rider gave him a package of letters. Swinging his knapsack to the ground, the young soldier broke the seals and hastily ran through the contents. One was from his guardian, Uncle Timothy Edwards, who, hearing of the boy's enlistment, now sent and ordered him to return. Others were from friends, who wrote in the most appealing manner, beseeching him to give up his wild resolve, as he would surely never come back alive. The lad turned defiantly to the horseman.

"Supposing I refuse to go back, how will you force me? If you should try, I would have you hung in ten minutes."

This staggered the messenger's hopes. Pleading was evidently useless here. He now produced

10

another letter.   This also was from the uncle, but
dropping the tone of command, he here lovingly
entreated the wandering youth to return to his
family, painting with a heavy hand the fearful suffering in the soldier's path, and the prospect of his
falling under the fatigue or the balls of the enemy.
But in case this letter, likewise, should fail, the
kind-hearted uncle sent gold, that his ward might
be well equipped.   The soldier-lad was moved to
tears, but he would not turn back.   He sent to his
uncle grateful and affectionate words, and explained
the noble motives which led him to this dangerous
service.   The messenger rode away ; the knapsack
was once more shouldered, and the determined
youth pushed on to the port of Newbury.

After a few days' halt at this ancient and beautiful
town, the little army sailed over the bar on the 19th
of September, and soon disembarked at Gardiner,
on the noble Kennebec.   Here two hundred bateaux were constructed, to carry these bold spirits
on their watery path through the wilderness.   Colonel Arnold sent forward two parties of scouts to
survey the Dead River and the Lake Megantic, and
the main body followed in four divisions, a day
apart, Morgan and his Virginia giants taking the
lead.   Soon the brave soldiers met the first hint of
the fearful hardships they were so gallantly entering.   As they worked their way up the calm river
there came first a rumble, then a roar,—and the

Norridgewock Falls suddenly lifted a towering wall of angry waters before the daring army. Undismayed, the troops landed, and with sturdy will began the herculean task. The banks of the river were steep and rocky; the gigantic forest-trees stood closely together, and the tumultuous speed of the waters so near the falls made the broad flatboats well-nigh unmanageable. For seven days the men tugged at the bateaux and staggered beneath their loads of stores and provisions,—transporting everything for over a mile through the dense forest to the smooth waters above. For seven days, above the unceasing roar of the falls, rose the merry shouts of the hardy pioneers, as with light hearts and heavy burdens they overcame the obstacles of nature. Active, and full of courage, our young soldier bore his share of the struggle, and encouraged his comrades by his impetuous zeal. His was a slight, frail form, but five and a half feet in height; yet he came from the hardiest of old Puritan stock, and his powers of endurance were wonderful. His smooth, boyish face and slight figure had won from the army the sobriquet of "Little Burr"; but his high courage and indomitable will had also won the admiration of all, while his generous nature stole the hearts of the entire band.

The boats had been strained by hard usage, a part of the provisions had spoiled, and soon after

the fresh start on the Kennebec, the Carratunc
Falls came in sight, and the same fatiguing delay
was again endured. The perils and privations had
but begun. The little army had now left behind
the last trace of civilization, and was fairly launched
upon as terrible a journey as ever an army performed. For thirty-two days they found no sign
of a human being. Lofty falls, impassable rapids,
impenetrable swamps, were constantly thronging
their course, and more than thirty times did they
carry the boats and stores around unconquerable
barriers, over rocky precipices, through the dense
forest and tangled brakes. As they advanced up
the river the stream grew rapid; often the oars
were useless, and poles would not stem the current,
and for much of the way the men were forced to
wade to their necks in water and push the boats
before them.

At length the Dead River was reached; but one-
fifth of the army had sunk beneath the fearful toil.
Once afloat upon the Dead River there was prospect of an easy passage. The stream flowed
smoothly on, through as grand a forest as ever
lifted its broad arms to the sun, and now the first
frosts of autumn had lighted the gloom with
gorgeous hues. Here and there a waterfall still
obstructed the way, but the carrying-places were
short, and the sturdy troops made merry sport of
the work. One day, a sudden bend in the river

brought into view a lofty mountain, lifting its snow-clad summit high above the forest. Here the troops encamped for three days ; then once again set forward, full of hope and courage. But a great disaster was gathering overhead. The long-threat-ening sky soon broke into a fearful tempest. The soldiers were encamped on the banks of the narrow river. In a few hours of darkness the floods poured down the ravines, and swelled the river till it rose eight feet; seven bateaux were overturned, and the provisions lost, and the poor men had little time to save themselves ere the whole plain was under the flood. It was thirty miles yet to the Chaudière River, which was to bear the army to the walls of Quebec, and scarce twelve days' provisions were left. Gloom and despondency entered these brave hearts, and terror made its first appearance in the camp. Starvation now showed its fearful visage, and stalked triumphant among the ranks. As yet, however, the remaining provisions served for short allowance, and the worst days had not fully come.

Through all these trying scenes " Little Burr" was foremost to do and to bear. When in college he had trained himself to eat but lightly, and this discipline now made his hardships less. In former years he had spent much of his time in boating, and his skill now became invaluable. His boat led the van of one division, and when a dangerous passage came in view, he took the helm himself,

10*

where his quick courage, keen eye, and steady hand won the enthusiastic admiration of the voyagers. One day he stood thus at the helm, when he saw the men who had been walking ahead on the shore running back toward the boats and throwing their arms wildly in the air. The boat was running some rapids, and the young helmsman could not shoot her in toward the shore. The boiling waters drowned the cries from the bank, and though the boy felt some danger was ahead, he could not learn its nature. Suddenly the terrible roar of a cataract fell upon the men's ears and blanched their faces with terror. The slight form at the helm did not quail; the blazing eyes were fixed upon the treacherous course ahead; like a bubble the fierce torrent hurled the great boat onward; for a second it trembled on the edge of a yawning gulf; the prow drooped, the stern lifted this one frail figure high into the air, and plunged into the roar and smoke twenty feet below. The boat upset, half the baggage was lost, one man sank in the tumult of angry waters, and "Little Burr" struck out for the shore, which he barely reached at last, overcome with fatigue and the icy waves.

Before the little army had left the Dead River the first breath of a northern winter covered the waters and chilled the hearts of the struggling band. The last part of the river-passage was made by wading through water and pushing the boats, while the ice gathered steadily about their track. In the last week of October, dragging the boats and few remaining stores through heavy snow, this handful of hardy and daring patriots passed over the high land which turns the rivers on one hand into the New England waters, and on the other into the St. Lawrence; launched upon a little stream flowing northward, and soon entered the broad Lake Megantic, whence flows the Chaudière to Quebec. From this point Arnold pushed rapidly ahead with a few picked men to reach the French settlements down the river and obtain provisions for the starving army, which he left to follow him as best they could. Before the succor arrived, however, the troops were upon the last verge of starvation. The stores were all gone, the last ox killed; even the faithful dogs that had followed their masters on this fearful march had been eaten, entrails and all, and the men were boiling their moccasins, with the hope of finding some nourishment, when a line of cattle drawing flour and provisions emerged from the woods, sent back by the indomitable colonel. Soon the separate divisions of the army met at Sertigan, and the battle with the wilderness was over. Through six hundred miles of wild, inhospitable forest, this devoted band had fought its way, and now, as the long-separated comrades met and clasped each other's necks, the joy of meeting was told with dim eyes and quivering lips, for half those gallant hearts who followed the drum and fife into the startled wilderness were with them no longer.

This sad reduction of his force made it necessary for Arnold to communicate with General Montgomery before he could begin operations against Quebec. But Montgomery was at Montreal, one hundred and twenty miles distant. Who would be willing to brave one hundred and twenty miles more of winter wilderness, with the horrors of the past forty days still clinging to the emaciated body? There was *one*, and Colonel Arnold's eye had been upon him through these trying scenes, noting well his high courage, his shrewd sense, his quick wit, his unconquerable will and power of endurance. "Little Burr" was summoned to the commander's tent. Arnold told him his dire necessity. The young soldier responded eagerly, proud of being intrusted with so dangerous a service. His course would lie through the enemy's country, accordingly he took no letter, but set out, alone, to carry a verbal message to the gallant young Montgomery at Montreal, which he had snatched from the British grasp. With subtle ingenuity, the young courier laid his plan of action. He clothed himself as a priest, and, relying upon the hatred of the French Catholics for their British rulers, hastened at once to a convent, and asked

for the spiritual chief. Burr remembered the
Latin he had acquired at college, and he was also
able to pronounce it with the French accent.
When the aged father appeared, the pretended
priest searched his face with unerring eyes, and
saw at once he was dealing with a man who could
be won. He boldly confessed his business, threw
himself upon the generosity of his host, and sought
his aid and advice. The venerable saint stood
aghast at the boy's daring. He eloquently painted
the perils of the journey, the terrors of the savage
wilderness, the impossibility of success, were so
slight a form to brave the untamed wilds. The
lad only smiled at all this; the memory of the past
days made the present enterprise seem light to his
mind. When the good man found that his strange
guest was not to be turned aside, he opened to him
a heart made warm and tender by a long life of
piety in the forest solitudes; he furnished a faithful guide, with such poor conveyance as he had;
and the dauntless boy set forth again, rejoicing.
On they moved through the forest, finding here
and there a kindly welcome from the French
priests who had erected their altars in these woodland depths, and meeting with no obstruction till
they reached Three Rivers. Here the people were
alarmed by the news of Arnold's march toward
Quebec, and the officers were determined to prevent any message from passing between his camp

and Montreal. "Little Burr" was eager to push on
and run the gauntlet, but the guide had no desire to
be captured, and insisted upon seeking the friendly
shelter of the French convent. Here the two
travelers lay concealed for three days. By that
time the excitement had died out, and they proceeded without molestation. Arriving safely at
Montreal, Burr went at once to the quarters of the
brave young Irish general. Montgomery was delighted with the news of Arnold's arrival, and
roused to great admiration by the wonderful courage and ability of the boy-courier. The generous
commander immediately offered Burr a position
on his staff. It was accepted, and this slender
youth received his first appointment,—captain and
aide-de-camp to Major-General Richard Montgomery. The general at once pushed forward through
blinding snows with his handful of hardy soldiers,
and reached *Point aux Trembles* on the first day of
December. Here were encamped the troops of
Arnold, who had already made several attempts
upon the garrison of Quebec. Montgomery took
command of the combined forces, numbering less
than a thousand men, and, setting forth in a fierce
snow-storm, the little army encamped against the
impregnable city.

A council of war was immediately held, at which
"Little Burr" and his young friend Ogden were
both present. It was agreed to carry the fortress

by storm! Think of the brilliant daring of this
little "army," less than a regiment in size, and
weakened by the terrible sufferings of that desert
march! The desperate attempt was just suited
to the mind of our hero. He begged to lead the
assault, and his request was granted. Forty men
were given him as a forlorn hope. With keen insight he picked the men who would never flinch,
—sturdy fellows who would revel in the work.
He put them at once to the most severe drill: he
had scaling-ladders constructed, and practiced his
men in mounting them on the run, loaded down
with all their marching equipments.

For two weeks he rested neither night nor day,
nor allowed rest to his soldiers. Every night he
exercised them in the use of their ladders, and
then walked alone beneath those iron heights,
which must be carried, studying every point and
preparing himself for the fearful assault. At the
last moment the plan was abandoned, and the disappointed aide always charged to this change the
failure of the expedition.

During this fortnight of waiting before the frown-
ing city, provisions fell short in the American camp.
"Little Burr" had only one biscuit and one onion
left.

One day he went down to a little stream to sat-
isfy his cravings by a draught of water. He had
no cup, and was just about to scoop up water with

his cap, when a British officer approached the brook on the other side and courteously offered his hunting-cup. The little captain gracefully accepted the kindness, and the two hostile officers fell into a friendly conversation. When the British officer turned back to the city he gave his new acquaintance a welcome piece of meat. Having learned each other's names, they stepped into the middle of the brook, shook hands warmly, agreed to remember one another should they meet again, and separated, as they supposed, forever. Thirty-six years after this pleasant event, Aaron Burr, hurled from a towering position in the hearts of his countrymen, cast down from the height of glory to a depth of degradation, and wandering among the bleak hills of Scotland, an outcast and an exile from home, met this old Scotch officer in his peaceful retreat. The old man took him warmly to his heart, and gave him the most valuable aid.

But the romance was not yet ended. A quarter of a century rolled on. The noble Scotchman was in his grave, and Aaron Burr, old and forsaken by his friends, was dying in New York. A daughter of that British officer, of that Scottish host, sought out the sick and lonely man, brought him into her own home, and soothed the last hours of the fallen giant.

Though the plan of the assault upon Quebec was changed, the assault itself was not abandoned.

It was determined to await a stormy night, and rush upon the garrison.

Meanwhile, the fierce Canadian winter closed in, the smallpox broke out in the camp, and the waiting troops were dwindling in numbers and wasting their strength upon the bitter air. Night after night the lonely sentry paced his round and watched for the longed-for storm.

The year 1775 was drawing its last gasps. The last night of December had opened with a flood of unclouded moonlight. It was evident that the slumbers of the troops would be unbroken. But soon the eager eyes of the sentinel saw huge black clouds driving across the sky, and suddenly a terrific snow-storm burst over the camp. The guard called the general from his sleep. "Little Burr" was at once aroused and dispatched to the division commander with orders to prepare in haste for the assault. The young aide examined the equipments of his own brave forty, saw that everything was in order, and waited impatiently for the word to advance. At five o'clock in the morning the magic word "Forward!" passed through the ranks. Through the raging storm the gallant men strode on to as desperate an attempt as ever stirred the blood of a soldier. "Little Burr" marched beside his general, followed by his forty, who led the first division. In a few moments the jagged steeps of Cape Diamond loomed up through the storm;

F   11

at the summit were the enemy's cannon. The first obstruction was a row of pickets: the storming party tore them up; on again, not seeing a rod in advance, eyes and ears filled with the driving snow. A second row of pickets! Fiercely the brave men tugged and hacked, for just beyond was the first outwork of the enemy, and every heart burned for the assault.

Montgomery, with his own hands, helped by his aides, Cheeseman, McPherson, and " Little Burr," worked at the obstructions.

At this moment the guard at the block-house first took the alarm, fired their muskets, and fled without discharging their cannon. The city would now be aroused! Every moment was priceless. Huge masses of ice were piled by the falling river around the pickets. Officers and men worked with fierce force. At last two hundred men had scrambled around and over and formed inside the pickets. Montgomery was still in advance, and beside his giant form was the slight figure of "Little Burr."

No need of secrecy now; they were discovered.

" Men of New York," thundered that deep voice above the roar of the storm, "you will not fear to follow where your general leads! Push on; Quebec is ours!"

These were his last words!

On rushed the devoted band. There came a terrible roar of cannon, and the tall form of Mont-

gomery fell forward upon the snow. Cheeseman
and McPherson dropped by his side, and only
" Little Burr" was left of the officers that so gallantly led that fearful charge ; the column wavered
and broke, appalled at the sweep of death; officers
counseled retreat; only the young aide still retained
his unfailing courage, and urged another onset. It
was too late. Fear seized the men, and as the cannon again blazed out through the darkness, the
ranks fled in wild confusion.

Not a thought given to the heroic leader, whose
glorious body lay dead in the drifting snow ? Yes;
"Little Burr" was not the one to leave his general
thus. While the grape-shot shrieked and howled
through the deserted waste, he stooped and swung
the majestic body upon his shoulders. *Then* he
turned his back upon the enemy's walls, and staggered beneath the precious load toward a place of
safety. British soldiers now rushed from the block-
house. On through the deep drifts, waist-high in
snow, the boy ran and stumbled under the heavy
weight. What glorious courage was there ! what
noble motives ! But the enemy rapidly gained ;
they were close upon him. Sadly he gave up the
unequal strife. He left the beloved form in the
snow, and barely escaped with his own young life.

Let not the glorious nobleness of this night's
deeds be forgotten whenever we reflect upon the
sad after-years of his fallen greatness.

The boy's part in that awful march through the wilderness and in the glorious night-assault on Quebec won for him at the time a generous appreciation. Arnold made him at once his brigade-major.

A few weeks later he returned to New York, and our last glimpse of the boyhood of Aaron Burr shows him, at the age of twenty, covered with honor, an aide-de-camp on the staff of Washington, commander-in-chief of the American armies.

THE VOLUNTEER AGAINST QUEBEC.

WHEN Arnold's expedition against Quebec had reached Fort Western, on the passage up the Kennebec River, the brave little army of eleven hundred stood upon the edge of a vast wilderness whose gloomy depths were almost wholly unsounded by the foot of man. The commander alone had even the faintest knowledge of the vastness and terrors of the savage wilds which lay in the path of the expedition.

It was necessary, therefore, to send forward a party of scouts, to mark the course which the troops should pursue, and to discover the rise and course of the Chaudière, which would bring the army to the walls of Quebec. Surveying his corps of officers, comprising some of the most gallant and efficient of those who became famous during the war, Arnold's choice fell upon Lieutenant Steele, a young man of great self-reliance and high courage. Of the eight soldiers chosen to accompany Steele on this desperate duty, one was John Joseph Henry, a boy of sixteen, and the youngest soldier in Arnold's army. Two guides skilled in river-craft and acquainted with a part of the route were obtained, and the little party, full of courage and in high spirits, set forth in two birch canoes upon their arduous journey.

Paddling on at the rate of about twenty miles a day, the last of September brought them to the great twelve-mile carrying-place.

Here ended the guides' knowledge of the country. Hundreds of miles yet lay before them, every step of which was a leap in the dark. Far behind them lay the last traces of civilization. Before them was a vast unknown. From fear that bands of Indians might be seeking a hunting-ground in these woodland wilds, the commander now ordered that no rifle should be discharged for any purpose, and no fire should be built by day or night. From time to time huge moose-deer looked with startled eyes upon the scouts, and flocks of wild ducks rose from the water, disturbed by the approaching paddles. But though the men were now in need of fresh meat, they were forced to depend alone upon angling for trout and chub, of which the streams were full.

Although the guides had never passed beyond the twelve-mile portage, one of them, Getchel, had heard from others of the course of the Dead River, and knew that its nearest point was a dozen miles away. Shouldering the canoes and provisions, the men struck out boldly over the rugged path, blazing the way with their tomahawks as they proceeded. The first day's march brought them to a little lake, whose clear waters were lively with trout. Here a council was held, and it was decided to leave one of the soldiers, Clifton, who was old and suffering from the severe fatigue. A companion, McKonkly, was allowed him; and for their sustenance till the return of the rest, which, they expected, would be within eight or ten days, one-half of the provisions were left behind.

In the morning Lieutenant Steele called about him the men who were to go on, including the boy, and distributed the remaining food in a manner to secure the strictest justice. The provisions were divided by the officer into equal portions, then ordering one of the party to turn his back, the lieutenant laid his hand upon one lot, and asked, "Whose shall this be?" The man answered at hap-hazard, calling any name that came to mind; and as he could not see the lot, it follows that impartiality was secured.

The diminished party set forward, and toward evening of the third day the Dead River glimmered through the forest.

Arrived at the banks, the evening meal too plainly spoke of the desperate situation to which the scouts were already reduced. It had been agreed that the pork should be eaten raw hereafter,

and only twice a day; and now, with a terrible
stretch of desert before them, they were forced to
be satisfied with only half a biscuit and half a
square inch of pork for a meal. But their courage
was still undismayed, and the scant repast was en-
livened with joke and laugh.

The next morning they awoke to a wilderness
of snow. This early advent of winter was startling
to the Southrons, as several of the men were from
Virginia, and gave added strength to their arms
when, launching the canoes upon the strange Dead
River, they struck out against the stream. Thirty
miles of watery course earned the wearied bodies
a sound night's sleep on the branches of the fir
and spruce.

The forest was a wonderful hunting-ground. As
the party moved on, drove after drove of stately
moose-deer passed them within range; and, when
a sudden turn in the river brought them close upon
a herd of gigantic fellows knee-deep in water, the
commander yielded to fiery pleading, and permitted
the men to shoot. The first gun flashed; the astonished deer threw their antlers high into air, and
dashed for the shore. Our boy-scout hastened to
fire, but the prey was already out of range, and
as the crack of his rifle died away through the
forest, the poor men had the painful reflection that
they had risked discovery and gained nothing
by it.

In the afternoon they came to a stream which descended from the northwest, and while they were debating which course to pursue, they discovered a stake driven into the ground near the water's edge, with a roll of birch-bark stuck in its cloven top. Hurriedly opening the roll, they found a beautifully drawn map of all the surrounding streams and water-courses, the portages, and the paths from stream to stream through the woods. This happy discovery lightened their cares, and with freer hearts they once more stemmed the current. They soon entered shoaler water; paddles were laid aside, and each man pushed at the poles, until a few days of uneventful labor brought them to the first pond at the head of the Dead River. A few cranberries here were greeted with shouts of joy,—ripe delicious cranberries as large as a cherry. Pond after pond stretched before them, for they were entering the highlands, and the rocky ridges broke the river into shallow pools.

An early start the next morning brought the scouts into a considerable lake, encircled with lofty mountains which reared their jagged sides straight out of the water. The air was bitterly cold, and when, at noon, the sun hid behind the snow-topped peaks, the little lad suffered intensely, though pad- dling with might and main. The close of day led them to the farther shore of the fifth and last lake, and they knew their forward journey was at an end.

F*

It only remained now to climb those forbidding
mountains, and read the open chart of the northward country beyond. The canoes were drawn to
shore and covered well with boughs and leaves.
Then the half-frozen men began the hard ascent,
and five miles of climbing and stumbling brought
them, well warmed at last, to the towering summit
of the loftiest mountain. The turbulent Chaudière
tumbled and boiled on its tortuous way at their
feet.

But the faithful lieutenant was not content with
this noble performance of a terrible task. Select-
ing the tallest pine, which shot up into the biting
air free of branches for forty feet, he called for the
nimblest climber, and soon, from a dizzy height,
came down a skillful description of the wild country
that stretched northward toward Quebec. Lake
Chaudière was the farthest point in sight.

With light hearts the brave little band stood
upon that peak, in the awful solitude of the untamed wilderness. Thousands of miles from home,
hundreds from the last verge of civilization, which
they had passed on the way, without provisions
and in a hostile country, they were yet happy in
the thought of a gallant service faithfully performed, in the consciousness of a victory far more
arduous and glorious than that won 'mid the roar
and smoke of battle.

In the thrill of that joyous moment, our little

lad of sixteen, who had run away from his father's home in Pennsylvania to join the camp at Cambridge, felt fully repaid for all his extreme sufferings of body and mind. Those few short weeks had earned for him the glorious title of *a man.* The future opened before him with a glowing light. He would carve his way to fame and to the admiration and gratitude of his country. Alas for the hopes of youth!

The scouts now set their faces to the return; set their faces toward the fearful stretch of winter wilderness; set them, unconsciously, toward far more appalling sufferings than they had yet endured.

The sun had fallen—night hastened on. Dense clouds were gathering overhead, and the thought of the approaching storm drove the men into a keen run. Indian fashion, they ran in single file, covering the track with their feet, lest some Canadian from over the mountain should discover their presence. Faster and faster they wound in and out on their flying descent. When half-way down the mountain the storm suddenly broke upon them in terrific fury. The rain soon swept down the slope in floods, and nearly carried their feet from under them. Night had closed in. The darkness was so dense that each man could scarcely see his leader. They came to a point where the path hung upon the very edge of a lofty precipice, and far below they heard the roaring of a swollen torrent.

They ran no more; they crept almost breathlessly inch by inch. A root caught the buckle of the lad's shoe; he lost his balance, fell over the cliff, and began a fearful descent. *He* thought into eternity, and so thought his comrades. An exclamation of horror,—it was all they could do. They could give no help; and no cry came up from the horrid roar and darkness of the abyss to tell them he was still alive. Far down the precipice a jutting rock threw out the twisted roots of a clump of pines. Into this little shelter the senseless body rolled. When time and the drenching rain brought the poor boy back to consciousness, his first thought was for his rifle. It was in his hand, unbroken, unharmed!

Dazed, stiff with wounds and cold, he started to crawl to the landing-place. He hardly knew where he was; he certainly did not know the exact direction, and to wander long meant simply to die. Our little scout was not ignorant of woodcraft. More than two years before, when fourteen years of age, he had made desperate journeys alone through the Indian-haunted forests on the western frontier. Groping along the steep side, clinging to the jagged rocks, with every sense now on the alert, he came at last to the path. An hour's intense exertion on bruised and bleeding feet brought him to the camp, where his comrades welcomed him as one from the dead. Under a wigwam of fir-boughs they slept, supperless and drenched to the skin.

And this was the beginning of the return !

Before daylight the heroic voyageurs were awake. The storm still raged, but their hearts yearned toward the south, and nothing could induce them to tarry. They slid the canoes into the lake, and grasped once more the paddles. Our bruised lad took a first turn at the labor, for he was stiff with wounds and nigh to perishing with cold. The canoes flew over the tumult of waters, and when day broke through the falling torrents, they had left the mountains far astern. Now the comrades looked into each other's eyes, and each one understood the look. They were hungry; they would break their fast; but *how?* Every man knew what he had in his pocket; each one had the same ; and yet, with the desperation of hope, that cruel toying with the feelings in which men indulge when hope has fled, each one began to overhaul his pouches, to fumble in every pocket, to search every nook. The result was that which they foreknew,—one solitary biscuit and one square inch of pork to a man ! And this on the very threshold of a winter desert, stretching hundreds of miles between them and the army.

They looked again one upon another, and without a word each one breakfasted upon one-half of a small biscuit. Their thoughts nerved their arms to greater strength and skill. The skiffs actually leaped over the lakes. One after another was quickly left behind, for there were no portages now between the sheets of water. The floods covered everything. At the last lake a diver was seen within range. The best shot in the party drew a bead on the fowl. How many prayers followed that ball! It struck and killed! The canoe was driven to the floating prize, which was eagerly grasped; again the skiffs headed on their course, and unceasing labor at the paddles brought them, when night set in, more than forty miles on their way. A fire was immediately built,—what cared they for Indians? Hunger was a stronger master than fear. A council was held. It was decided that each man's piece of pork should be placed in the kettle with the duck; the broth should be the supper, and the fowl kept for breakfast. Gloomily the men sipped their pitiable allowance; gloomily they passed a comfortless night. In the morning the duck was divided by the commander, each man greedily watching to ensure fair proportions; then one of the party turned away his face, and "whose shall this be?" decided the portion of each starving man. The boy Henry was very fortunate, and drew a thigh. He needed it. He felt the wasting of strength insidiously conquering his powers, but he kept his knowledge to himself.

That day they made fifty miles. They talked of soon meeting the army, and as they talked their courage increased and their hopes grew brighter. In their night encampment they made no fire. They ate the bits of pork saved from the broth, and the remaining half-biscuits. It was the last morsel in the party. For the first time they were totally without food!

All day they traveled without speaking a word. The appalling silence of those solitudes was unbroken, save by the dipping paddles and the sighing of the keen winter wind through the pines. They slept supperless; they started in the morning breakfastless. The heavy floods had swollen the river, and the canoes were hurled swiftly down the stream, with masses of driftwood from the heights above, and immense trees which carried their threatening branches high above the water. Towards noon they saw a vast column of smoke ahead, spreading upward in the clear sharp air. Joy filled their hearts, for they felt they should soon meet the advancing army.

A huge tree lay in the middle of the stream, firmly rooted in the bed, and stretching its wide forks toward the banks. The first canoe, with the commander and Getchel, the guide, shot safely between the forking branches. When our lad's canoe drew near,—each man with a paddle,—an unlucky stroke was given, the skiff veered a little

from the true course; one scraggy prong seized
the light boat in the bows a few inches above the
water, and suddenly rent the whole side from stem
to stern. A horrible death rushed in through the
ghastly opening. Instinctively the men leaned
toward the other side. That movement saved their
lives. The gaping rent was lifted out of water.
Still in this position the men paddled carefully toward the shore, and landed near the rising smoke,
where they were joined by the other canoe. The
stillness of the spot chilled their hopes. They
rushed over a knoll,—all was desert solitude. No
army; not a living soul. It was only the place
where they had built a fire on the passage up, carefully covering it that no smoke might escape till
they should be far on their way. It had broken
through, crept into the surrounding turf, and the
smoke was now streaming up from half an acre of
burnt ground. Sadly they turned back to their
wrecked canoe and gloomy prospects.

The disabled skiff was laid on the side, the rent
examined, and every bag rummaged for a roll of
birch and a piece of pitch. In vain! All had been
used. Despair now seized upon the group. In the
depths of an inhospitable wilderness, without food,
without means of transportation! For the first
time they wondered where the army could be, and
the same thought pierced every soul,—it must have
returned to Boston! Only the guide, Getchel, did

not sink. Pacing thoughtfully a few moments, he sent one into the forest for birch-bark, and went himself to seek for turpentine. Our lad, with the buoyancy of youth, recovered his spirits and soon returned with salvation in his hands. Suddenly the black cloud again shut down. What should they do for oil, to turn the turpentine into pitch? While the impossibility of relief was talked over, the boy chanced to think of the empty pork-bag, yet lying in the whole canoe. It was brought, turned inside out, carefully scraped, and every crumb gathered as if it were dust of gold; more anxiously, for what would gold avail in this desert? Cedar-roots furnished the ropes, the canoe was repaired, and two hours after the men committed their rescued lives once more to the rushing river.

Not venturing, at first, into deep water, the wounded canoe followed the shore. A quarter of a mile from the last landing, little John Henry at the helm, the skiff ran upon a hidden snag, which thrust its ugly snout up through the bottom. Pushing a coat-sleeve into the hole, there was no alternative but to put back to the old fire, and again mend the ill-fated craft. This took another hour. But fate had not yet worked its perfect work. As the men were bearing the canoe once more to the river, having reached the brink of the bank, the forward lifter slipped, the canoe fell from his hands and broke completely open in the middle. There it lay in two pieces; around it stood the men, with hope now at the lowest ebb.

Over our young soldier's heart came a feeling of deathly sickness. Unutterable despair took full possession of his soul. He felt assured that God had led him there to the wilderness to die a cruel death. Led him there? Ah, no! This was the bitterest thought of all; he had led himself to this awful hour. The happy life of his childhood, his wickedness in deserting a loving home, the cruel pain and anguish of his tender parents and sisters as time rolled on and no tidings came of the cherished, wayward boy,—all these rushed upon his mind and overwhelmed his soul with agony. He turned his face, while the bitter, burning tears streamed down his cheeks, and from that hour his heart ever went forth to his loved ones with a yearning tenderness he had never felt before.

But meanwhile Getchel, the guide, was as determined as fate, and apparently as unconquerable. The two parts of the skiff were instantly set together, and strongly sewed with the roots of cedars; melted pitch was thickly poured over the whole seam; over that was drawn a wide roll of bark, reaching under the canoe from gunwale to gunwale, and still over this was stretched the ripped pork-bag, which, being saturated with fat, would well keep out the water. It was now nearly dark, but the unanimous desire was to push on.

The canoes were launched, and the men plied the paddles with a will.

They had now been three days without a morsel of food. Their strength was rapidly sinking, and their eyes burned with that cruel glare of hunger which is so terrible to look upon. Just as dusk stole out from the forest and began to settle upon the river, the lieutenant's canoe being out of sight around a bend, the sharp crack of a rifle broke suddenly upon the air, followed instantly by another, and then by a wild shout. "Indians!" thought our lad, and so guessed the others. They made the canoe fairly leap as they rushed forward to defend their comrades. The next moment, as they shot round the bend, they saw rescue, salvation, *life itself,* falling from a cliff and rolling toward the river,—an enormous moose! They were not weak *then!* At least, no one would have thought it, as they sent up a shout that rang away through the forest. Steele had caught a glimpse of the giant beast, and quickly brought him down. The canoes flew to the shore; a fire was soon crackling and roaring, the nose and lip cut off, and the starving men fell upon a feast not only of great plenty, but also of rare delicacy. After these choice parts were eaten, the whole night was spent in preparing the prey for carriage, and—who could help it?— tasting of every nice bit.

At daybreak they snatched a little sleep, and

when the sun burst through the trees they were again on their feet, ready to advance with light hearts, for they felt that they had now reached the hunting-grounds, and their sufferings were past.

The night of October 13th found the voyagers at their first camp on the Dead River, where, more than three weeks before, they had slept on their journey northward. The small stock of fat was now consumed; for weeks they had eaten no bread or vegetables, and the terrible strain and suffering had previously so weakened them, that lean meat alone was insufficient for their needs. As they looked upon one another and took counsel with their own hearts, they saw too plainly that the unequal contest was likely to end in but one way.

They reached this old camp just after noon. The whole party was in so reduced a state that it was felt to be impossible to transport the canoes across the twelve-mile carrying-place; they did not attempt even to drag them from the water. They fastened them to the shore by stout withes, then slowly and painfully carried their arms and baggage up the steep bank. They at once proceeded to jerk the moose-meat.

As soon as it was hung over the smoke-fires, the scouts sat down to discuss their situation. It was far from hopeful. They had been expecting for several days to meet the army, and were now forced to the conviction that it had returned, to the belief that they were deserted, left alone to die of hunger in this dreadful wilderness. The idea of carrying the canoes to the Kennebec over the twelve-mile portage was not entertained for a moment. It was a physical impossibility. They decided to rest here till the meat was jerked, which would take six days, when, if still living and able to crawl, they would walk to the Kennebec and—well, they would know better then what they *could* do. Across the twelve-mile portage, nearly to the great river, was the spot where they left Clifton and McKonkey on their passage northward; but they had not strength enough now to search for their comrades. Steele, the commander, was hardly satisfied to lie still six days, and it was finally determined that he should take Getchel and another man, and go over afoot to the Kennebec to look for the army, promising to return in three days whether they found it or not. After they left, the poor fellows who remained at the Dead River were more despondent than ever. Especially our lad, John Joseph Henry, found that his scarce sixteen years of life had not gathered endurance sufficient to bear sufferings which were breaking down the hardiest pioneers. He ate meat many times a day, never satisfied, constantly growing feebler. Meat alone, without bread, vegetables, or salt, could not repair the wasted tissues. His mind became too weak to resist the terrible cravings of the stomach; he ate inordinately of the moose, and induced a diarrhœa that sapped his remaining strength.

Day after day went by; it was now the fourth night since the commander had left, yet the forlorn hope did not return. On the next morning a council was held, but the majority, given over to despair, voted to remain rather than to struggle on, with the certainty of perishing.

Young Henry was disposed to made another desperate fight for rescue. It seemed to him that the army *must* be on the way; he could not finally believe himself to be abandoned by God to a horrible death. He induced Sergeant Boyd to join him in one more effort. Henry was the youngest soldier in Arnold's army,—Boyd was the strongest. The lad, almost too weak to move about, pleaded for the strong man's help and got it. They took the best canoe and feebly paddled into the neighboring creek till they reached the point nearest the first pond on the portage. Here they landed and proceeded on foot, hoping against hope to find the vanguard of the army.

They soon reached a bog which must be passed. Just after entering it, Boyd dragged himself to a log and threw himself upon it, exhausted. The strong man had failed,—failed in body and mind. His heart was broken down, his splendid courage gone. The lad tried, with a ruggedness of spirit wonderful in one of his years, to rouse again the manly soul. Forgetful of his own excruciating sufferings, he essayed to lift the sergeant to his feet. The crushed man put forth no effort. The lad then poured into his ears the watch-words he so well knew were the most stirring to a soldier's soul,— home, wife, children, courage, honor! The poor man answered only by a flood of tears. The body had sunk, and dragged with it mind and soul. Then the boy turned aside his face and prayed. For over an hour the two sat there without a word. The winter wind caught their sobs, and sighed away through the forest. Their tears froze where they fell. So their lives were passing into pitiless void, with no eye to see, no heart to feel, their agony.

Ah! there was an Eye and a Heart! The God of the wilderness was there. The uttermost parts of the earth were His, and His hand was over all the works which He had made. He brought back the youngest soul to hope and courage. Then the lad turned softly to the sobbing man and pleaded with him to return to their comrades. Mechanically the soldier rose, the brave boy helped him to the skiff, and they returned to the camp.

That night despair filled every heart. Out through those long, dark hours each soul might have fled, without ever a prayer to stay. But the morning light was precious, and when the sun rose gloriously over the forest they felt that life was worth another struggle. They determined to cross the portage to the Kennebec, and perish, if they must, upon the way. They went up the creek in the canoes, left them behind forever, and set forth on foot. They were too weak to walk erect; they stumbled over every root and twig; if a man fell he had not strength to rise alone. They reached the bog where yesterday God had spoken to the young boy's soul. To-day He appeared in a far more glorious manner. Just as they were arousing their courage to attempt the passage, the crash of axes, the shouts of men, fell suddenly upon their ears! The next moment appeared, beyond the bog, the vanguard of the army, pioneers making a causeway for the troops. A feeble cry of joy went up from the rescued; strength seemed suddenly to enter their limbs; they boldly plunged into the swamp, gained the farther side, and came out upon the astonished soldiers.

As the pioneers looked upon these emaciated forms, clasped the bony hands, gazed into the sunken eyes which glowed with the light of fearful sufferings, the tears rolled fast along their hardy cheeks. They gave the famished men some food, and told them that the advance-guard, under Major Febiger, lay at the next pond. They hurried on. The young lad, still stronger than his comrades, reached the camp-fire first. No one knew him. Febiger somewhat sternly demanded his

name and business. The unexpected answer completely overcame this noble man. His canteen
held the last drop of liquor in the army; quickly
and tenderly he put it to the boy's lips, and as one
after another of the rescued scouts came up, the
precious fluid passed around. This Danish soldier
was a man of great heart. He was overjoyed to
think he had the spirits to offer when he saw the
reviving of power beneath its influence. He seated
them around his fire, put on the kettle with pork
and dumplings (*bread and fat,*—how their eyes
glistened !), and set the life-giving food before
them with the tenderness of a mother.

While they were feasting, the great Morgan
came up with giant strides,—Morgan, destined to
be one of the greatest heroes of the war. With
stentorian voice he bade a rough and hearty welcome. Then came Steele and Getchel, and soon
our little lad was the centre of a riotous group,—
a hundred soldiers pressed around to hear his story
and hug him for very joy. The lieutenant now
explained why he had not returned according to
his promise. After reaching the army he fell beneath a heavy burden and dislocated his shoulder.
He then sent out men with supplies, but they returned without finding the party. It was all over
now ; four weeks of fearful suffering seemed light
in the joy of the present moment.

There were no "ambulances," no helps for the

"sick-list" in this desert-march; to be unable to keep pace with the army was simply to be left to die. Young Henry, therefore, worked on as best he could. Indeed, his spirit led him to forget his weakness and suffering, and he plunged into the coming struggle with wonderful ardor and courage. He was now to go over the same ground, but he did not expect the same trials. With the buoyancy of youth he painted bright pictures of the immediate future, and stretched forward for the glory which was to crown his labors. It was well for him—it was well for all that fated band—that the future unrolled itself only from day to day.

The next morning the first two divisions reached the scouts' old camp on the Dead River. Here they rested three days, until the rear of the army, the New England troops, had arrived. Then, pushing on, they advanced in boats and upon the riverbank, fighting their way against stream and forest.

A few days' travel brought the vanguard to the foot of the mountain from whose summit, weeks before, the scouts had looked over toward Canada.

The army now heard the news of Enos's desertion, and learned that the provisions were exhausted. The little that was left was equally divided, giving five pints of flour only to each man. And they were yet one hundred miles from the frontier of Canada!

A drifting snow soon closed around them, increasing their labors and sufferings. They were forced to break the ice with their muskets, as they waded through the swamps that beset their way.

Two women had followed their husbands through all this terrible journey, and on this day our lad passed one of them, a beautiful young girl, coaxing her exhausted husband to rise from the ground to which he sank in despair, and make another effort for life. It was a sad sight, but the end was sadder still. Toward night the troops reached Lake Chaudière,—now called Lake Megantic,— and hurriedly skirting its shores, they encamped at night-fall beside the outlet of the Chaudière River.

The morning found young Henry stiff with bruises and faint with hunger. But the drums beat forward, and there was no choice but to struggle on or perish in the wilderness. They came to a stream which must be crossed on a slippery tree that had fallen over the water. On they went in single file; it was dizzy work. One poor man just ahead of Henry slipped and fell into the foaming water. No hand was outstretched to save him, for it was impossible. The current swept him under, and he was gone.

The lad suffered terribly with his feet. His moccasins were long since worn out, and now the seam in the heel of his leather shoe had worked into a deep cut, and the pain was excruciating. There was nothing to do but to bear it. He could not stop to cast off the shoe or to bandage the wound, for the men pressed on, and if one got out of line his place was filled with the heartlessness of a machine. He would then have to wait for the rear, a position which every man dreaded. Towards noon Lieutenant Simpson, however, noticed the deathly look in the boy's face, and ordered a halt. The wound was dressed, the shoe fixed, and the march again went on. Late in the afternoon they found a dangerous cataract, and wondered how the boats had passed it. Soon they came to a group of soldiers sitting around a fire. They were the men who had gone on in the bateaux. The sad story was soon told. They were swept over the falls, lost everything but their lives, and one poor fellow, Lieutenant McClelland, was dying. He came, like Henry, from Pennsylvania, and when now he saw the lad, he beckoned to him. Stooping down to catch the poor man's failing breath, the lad heard one whispered word, " Farewell." They left him and marched on.

Coming to a sandy spot, the men detected a kind of root they knew to be edible. They immediately scattered in every direction, and tore them up and ate them, till the place was utterly stripped. At night the soldier-lad found some men building a fire under a kettle. Excited by wonder, for there were no provisions in the army, he came up to the fire. As he sat down on the end of a log, he upset the kettle. The starving men were so enraged that one of them would have shot him had not Simpson come up at that moment and interfered. The men now offered their "soldier's fare." It was broth of a greenish color, and they said it was a bear. But the truth soon leaked out. A noble Newfoundland dog, belonging to Captain Thayer, had been killed for food, amid the tears of the men, who appreciated his fidelity through the horrible march in the desert.

Starving though he was, our lad could not eat this. He cast himself on the ground, and gave way to the gloomiest thoughts. He would gladly have died at once. He did not want to struggle on any further, for he felt that death would be the end, and he was willing to die now. But the brave Lieutenant Simpson was cheering the camp by singing "Plato" on an empty stomach, and Henry soon regained his courage by this example of cheerfulness. For forty-eight hours the men had not tasted of food. They were now boiling their moccasins, hoping to get some nourishment from the mucilage. But after all the boiling it was leather still, and the men chewed it long and got no refreshment.

Hunger would not let them sleep, and before daylight they were again on the march. They tramped on gloomily in almost unbroken silence, for all were filled with misery, and cared not to talk. In the afternoon they suddenly descried, on turning a point of land, a heavily-laden boat far down the river. Every eye was strained, and it was soon seen to be approaching. In a few moments a more glorious sight appeared through the forest,—a large drove of cattle coming along the shore! They seemed to be not far away, and the men urged on their jaded powers, eager for the relief. But the bank wound in and out; there were numerous inlets around which the troops had to make long stretches; at times the cattle were lost to view, and it was only after several hours of hurried struggling that the starving men reached the spot where the cattle had been. There was not a thing to be found! There were a few Frenchmen standing around a decaying fire. These were Canadians whom Arnold, going ahead in a light boat to find succor for his army, had sent back through the forest with cattle for its use. They said that at this spot they were met by the first division of troops, the cattle were immediately slaughtered, cast upon the fires, and in a twinkling every morsel was greedily devoured. The poor soldiers had eaten even the entrails, many of them tearing these parts from the warm carcasses and devouring them raw. It was a bitter disappointment to our starving men, but they laid down to sleep with hopes that the morrow would bring their salvation.

The next day was John Joseph Henry's birthday,—his seventeenth. His thoughts naturally
turned back to the loved home far off in Pennsylvania, and he could but think of the contrast between his present condition and his surround-
ings in former years as the happy day came round.
His father, who had entered the army, where was
he ? His mother and sisters ! Oh, what yearnings
he felt to hear one word from the dear ones at
home ! But he did not regret his choice. His brave
and sturdy soul would not permit his mind to
waver, and he still kept pace with the rest, determined to share in the capture of Quebec or the
destruction of the army.

In the afternoon they forded a stream to the arm-
pits,—icy water from the winter hills. Emerging
on the farther bank, they saw through the woods
a house by the brink of the river. The first house
in Canada ! They hastened joyfully on, for they
felt sure of relief, sure of rescue from death by
starving. The kind-hearted French settlers brought
out their stores and set them generously before the
ravenous men. Then began a riotous scene of inordinate feasting ; meat, bread, potatoes, all disap-
peared as if by magic. All prudence, all the teach-
ings of experience, were forgotten or ignored. They
gorged themselves without stint. Some of them
escaped death by starvation only to fall victims to
their first meal. In a few hours our soldier-lad

looked upon the corpses of some of his own friends,
—men from his own county. Others were taken
violently sick and were saved only by desperate
remedies. Young Henry himself had remembered
the danger of inordinate indulgence, and he received strength and cheer from his own share of
the feast.

The next two days the army's route lay through
a low, rich country, dotted with houses and crosses
along the way. These signs of civilization rejoiced
the boy's heart. His perils seemed to be passed
in safety, the people showed themselves friendly,
and *Quebec* now filled every man's mind and
mouth.

At noon of the second day they reached the
camp of the commander, Benedict Arnold, and
learned that Quebec was thirty miles away. Lieutenant Steele, the leader of the scouting-party, had
become Arnold's aide, and another of our boy's
messmates was the colonel's commissary.

Henry went at once to headquarters, and was
directed by Steele to a slaughter-house, a hundred
yards distant. Here was Taylor dealing out the
beef in liberal measure,—every man took what he
wanted. For once the lad forgot his prudence,—
he overate, though he ate but little; in a short
time he was too sick to stand.

That night he lay in a farm-house. What a
luxury it was! Yet he could not sleep, but rolled

to and fro in agony. In the morning, however, he made a desperate effort and took his place in line. The army now marched in good order, for they had fair roads and easy traveling. The lad's pain and weakness increased, aggravated by his exertions, and about noon he fell out of line and sank upon a log. There he lay, seeing the troops march steadily by, feeling that he had conquered the wilderness only to die from his own misdoing. After the rear of the army came Arnold on horseback. The commander knew the sick boy, and was acquainted with his gallant service in the desert. He dismounted and asked kindly about his sickness. One glance at the boy's face was enough. Arnold hastily remounted, and dashed off to the nearest house. Soon a Frenchman came and carried him to the cabin. Henry gave his rifle in charge of a lagging soldier. Arnold placed two dollars in the lad's hands, and he was left in the Frenchman's care. In an hour he was in a raging fever.

In a few days he was able to leave, and he determined to set forth at once. The kind Canadian scornfully refused to receive any pay, but took the weak lad to the ferry, several miles off, and there got him a free passage to the other side. Here the track of the army was plainly seen. Mile after mile the poor boy trudged on alone, ready to sink from weakness, yet driven forward

G*

by a brave and restless heart. For ten miles he did not see a living thing; late in the afternoon he reached the camp, and immediately sought out his rifle. He was again a soldier.

The little army, dwindled to half its original size, was now at the end of its terrible march. From the camp at Point Levi the men saw far across the St. Lawrence the iron heights of Abraham and the towering walls of Quebec. They knew the city was poorly garrisoned, and they burned to rush on to the assault. But the British had heard of their approach through the wilderness, and every boat was withdrawn to the farther side of the river. Arnold sent far and near, and finally collected about forty birch canoes. Then a fearful storm broke over the camp; it raged three days, and while the Americans were compelled to keep their tents the garrison of Quebec was reinforced by troops from Sorel.

At length the storm cleared, the river subsided, and the troops crossed over in the night. Gathering on the enemy's shore, Colonel Arnold placed himself at the head of the skeleton army, and they scaled the ragged heights. At daybreak they formed in martial array on the broad plains of Abraham.

Here now stood this band of gallant spirits, without artillery, with half their muskets useless, before one of the most formidable fortresses in the world. It is almost impossible to conceive the courage and determination that led these patriot souls to hurl themselves against those iron walls. But they had come to take Quebec, and they cried now to be led to the assault. The time was not yet ripe. Arnold paraded his army before the city, and the crowds upon the parapets cheered it with derisive huzzas. The troops returned them, and some even crept toward the walls with the hope of picking off a few men with the rifle. The British discharged their cannon, but the balls fell short. Arnold withdrew his men, and from this day young Henry lost respect for his commander. He felt that the parade was a piece of bravado unbecoming a true soldier, and so, indeed, it was.

For two days the troops lay quietly in camp. The third day saw the first death by the enemy's fire. Our lad was one of a party sent across the river to buy some cattle. The British guns opened upon them, and the soldier who pulled next to Henry was shattered by a ball. He died in a short time, refusing to drink a bowl of tea from the kind hand of a Canadian woman, saying, with his last breath, "No, madam; it is the ruin of my country."

A week passed on, and Arnold, learning of the reinforcements to the city, ordered a retreat. This was discouraging work, and our lad's mind was filled with gloomy speculations. He could not know the commander's secrets; he only knew they were turning their backs upon the city they had come to conquer. Twenty miles they marched, beside the great St. Lawrence, through clumps of forest, past pleasant farm-houses, to the village of *Point aux Trembles.* Just before reaching the village a boat was seen flying swiftly down the river. The men did not then know that this skiff held Sir Guy Carleton, driven from Montreal by Montgomery, and now escaping to Quebec.

Here the army was distributed among the houses, the French people showing the men much kindness.

Our lad was quartered on a family whose two rosy daughters made the days pass pleasantly, and gave him the first taste of civilization he had had for months.

On the 1st of December, General Montgomery came from Montreal and took command of the combined forces, numbering less than nine hundred men. The next day they set out for Quebec in a raging snow-storm, which soon blocked their way with drifts.

For two weeks now the troops lay in sight of the city. The brave Irish general had determined to wait for a stormy night and carry the fortress by assault. The men were ignorant of the plan, and murmured greatly at the delay.

About the middle of the month the rifle com-

panies, to which young Henry belonged, were
moved nearer Quebec. The men often crept up
under the city walls and picked off sentries with
their unerring rifles; but this was the only excitement to break the weary waiting.

One day the beautiful young wife whom our lad
had seen encouraging her husband at the head
of the Chaudière, came into camp, bringing the
poor man's rifle and accoutrements. He had
died in the wilderness, and the brave woman had
struggled on alone, through weeks of suffering, to
join the army.

The riflemen were stationed at the most advanced posts, and our soldier-lad took his turn
with the rest. One night, on being relieved from
guard, he fell asleep on a bench in the guard-
house. This was a stone building, close by the
Palace Gate. The British began to shell the
pickets. Almost the first shot struck the stone
wall directly where Henry was leaning his head.
Three feet of wall kept the thirteen-inch shell on
the outside, but the terrific concussion woke the
boy and drove him, bewildered, out into the snow.
Unconscious of what he was doing, he plunged
through the snow, which was three feet deep,
and ran into a coal-shed, two hundred feet away.
Soon the biting cold recalled his senses and he
went back to the guard-house, having learned what
it means to be panic-stricken. On another night

he was on his beat near the Palace Gate. Suddenly a fearful howl broke the stillness, then a rush of many men, then the British cannon flashed through the darkness, and the shells shrieked and burst over the young lad's head.

Expecting an assault from the enemy, the guards fled, and the brave little fellow was left alone. He waited long for relief, but none came. Soon a band of men rushed out again with great noise, and the deserted sentry fled into a large garden. Atfer a while the shelling ceased, and, creeping out from his hiding-place, he ran two miles to the camp. Feet and hands were frozen, and were saved only by being plunged into snow and rubbed for hours.

At length the hour drew near for which these men had conquered six hundred miles of untrodden wilderness and borne sufferings unutterable.

The 30th of December was a cloudless day; at night the moon sailed forth into a cloudless sky. The troops fell asleep without a suspicion of the work before them, and the sentries paced their lonely rounds. Towards midnight huge clouds began to gather, the wind rose to a gale, and soon a furious snow-storm drove through the camp. Montgomery was on his feet in an instant, the men were aroused, silently marshaled, and silently they set forth to the attack. The snow cut their faces and blinded their eyes, but they rushed on, thinking of naught but victory.

The little army was divided into three divisions. Two under Montgomery and Morgan were to carry the lower town, while a third, from the Plains of Abraham, was to feign an attack on the upper city to draw off the British troops. Our lad was with Morgan. The riflemen plunged on, holding down their heads to keep their eyes from the cutting storm, and covering their gun-locks with the lappets of their coats. Drawing near the city, they ran in single file over a narrow path toward the Palace Gate. They entered between two rows of houses, a narrow street without the city. Here a terrible fire of musketry opened upon them. Noble fellows dropped in the snow,—their places were filled; the line kept on.

Still running at full speed, the boy-soldier was struck under the chin and knocked over a banking twenty feet high. Over and over he rolled, plunging into a snow-drift which completely overwhelmed him. His knee was injured by a cake of ice, his chin was bruised, he was nearly senseless. He grasped his rifle and dragged himself painfully up the bank. His company was far in advance; he was forced to fall in with strange men whom he had never seen before. His pain was excruciating, his head swam—he fell. Again the column swept on; again he recovered, forced himself into the line, and advanced to the charge. The shot poured from the lofty walls; brave men 'fell at every step.

Arnold now went past, borne wounded to the rear. The men saw him, caught his parting cheer, and rushed on. They came to the first barrier; they carried it. They dashed straight toward the blaze of the British cannon, plunged through the embrasures, captured and killed the whole guard. On they charged. A second barrier; this gave them hot work. Montgomery had been killed, his troops retreated, and the relieved defenders had hastened back to repulse Morgan.

Henry was with the riflemen again, hemmed in between two lofty walls, every shot from the ramparts raking through the crowded passage. Morgan ordered a charge. The barrier was of solid stone, twelve feet high. Against this merciless wall the men hurled themselves in fury. Cannon from the ramparts belched their terrible fire; the houses on every hand were ablaze with the flash of innumerable muskets. Once and again did this gallant band rush upon the deadly barrier and attempt to scale the height. Then out of this hell of roar and death rose the great voice of Morgan ordering the troops to take the houses. A furious onslaught followed; the houses were held by the rifle corps. From every window, then, they poured unerring bullets over the ramparts.

Daylight was breaking upon the terrible scene. The heavy shot from the enemy tore through the buildings, and here many a gallant soldier breathed his last. The havoc among the officers was fearful. Hendricks, Humphreys, Cooper, fell dead at nearly the same instant. Captain Lamb had his cheek shot away. Steele lost his fingers; nearly every one of our lad's own officers was killed or wounded.

They determined to retreat. It was too late. The enemy, seeing by the growing light their dangerous position, sallied forth from the Palace Gate, and now assailed them in the rear. Still the gallant riflemen kept up a splendid defense. Till nine in the morning they held the enemy at bay. Then Morgan heard of Montgomery's death, of the capture of Dearborn's men; he found himself left alone with his sturdy riflemen. The odds were too heavy, the end was certain; he would not sacrifice so many noble fellows,—he surrendered.

The glorious struggle was over. These gallant men had fought the old year out; they crossed the threshold of the new year, and the prison doors clanged behind their backs.

As soon as the officers gave up their swords they were led away to a seminary and imprisoned. The riflemen were then paraded in line, and Colonel McDougal, a Scotch officer, passed down

to examine them.   Young Henry knew him well,
having often met him at an uncle's in Detroit.
When the colonel asked the lad his name, the boy
mentioned this former acquaintance.   The British
officer seemed pleased at the memory, and the lad
at once asked to be sent to the officers' prison, to
be with his intimate friends.   But the kind-hearted
old colonel told him he had better stay with the
men, for the officers would probably be sent to
England and tried for treason.   The story of Ethan
Allen came across the young prisoner's mind, and
he gladly chose to follow the advice.   After this
review the prisoners were marched to the monastery of the *Reguliers.*   This was an immense building, and would hold four thousand men.   The
troops were led into the upper story ; here they
were crowded into small rooms, bare, cold, cheer-
less, and prison life began.

A pleasant occurrence, however, soon lighted
the gloom of this sad New Year's Day.   Some
generous merchants of Quebec obtained permission to make the captives a New Year's gift.
They sent in a large butt of porter and a quan-
tity of bread and cheese.   The poor fellows attacked these good things vigorously, determined
to be jolly in the midst of misfortune.   After all,
it was hard work.   The death-shrieks of their
slaughtered friends still rung in their ears, while
a thousand memories of far-off homes gathered

about them a weight of darkness. There was little
sleep that night, for all the terrible exhaustion.

On the third day a file of soldiers came to lead
our young prisoner to the seminary. Morgan
had heard of his desire to be with the officers,
and induced their captors to send for the lad. But
he had been struck with the good advice of the
Scotch colonel, and chose to remain in the convent.
On this day, also, the kind-hearted Carleton had
sent a flag of truce to Arnold to get the baggage
which belonged to the prisoners. Henry's did not
come, but there was an unclaimed knapsack, and
he seized that for his share. He got from it a large
blanket, which proved valuable in the coming days,
and a drummer's coat, which he afterward bartered.
On this day, too, the mournful funeral of Montgomery passed the convent windows, and the soldier-lad buried his face in his hands and shed bitter
tears of grief. Montgomery was the idol of his
soldiers. The next day saw still a sadder scene.
Cart after cart drove by the monastery, loaded
with the bodies of the slain patriots. The corpses
had frozen in the snow where they fell, and now
their limbs were fearfully distorted. The corridors
of the convent echoed with the sobs of the prisoners as this sad spectacle moved by. The bodies
were piled in a heap in the "dead-house," and left
till spring should open the ground.

The prisoners were now fairly settled in their

new life. Sir Guy Carleton had a kind heart, and so the allowance of food was sufficient for their needs. Each prisoner was given daily a biscuit of meal, a half-pound of pork, butter, molasses, vinegar, and candles. But young Henry's appetite was lively, and his allowance would not keep it quiet. His ingenuity soon helped him out of this difficulty. Lobscouse was a daily dish, and it was very difficult to manage without a spoon. But spoons were something the prisoners did not have. One day, however, our lad found a piece of hard wood among the pine fuel. He eagerly pounced upon it, and in a short time had shaped a wooden spoon. Then the men all wanted spoons, but the stick of wood belonged to the boy, the knife belonged to the boy, and the men gladly purchased his handiwork with biscuits. In this way he satisfied his hunger for some time.

In the dreary monotony of their life, the men soon fell to gaming. They had neither money nor clothes, but they staked their provisions, and oftentimes the excitement ran high. One jolly young sergeant, named Crone, was always in luck at gaming, and as he had an affection for Henry, he often gave him twenty or thirty biscuits at a time. So the boy's larder was kept full.

Toward the last of January the prisoners were removed to the Dauphin Jail. This was a spacious building, and their accommodations were better than at the monastery. The Dauphin Jail stood less than a quarter of a mile from the St. John's Gate. As the men looked out across the open space between the two, they began to think of escape. The windows were heavily barred, but the sentries were always on the outside, and the provost-captain was a kind, unsuspicious man. The guard at the gate usually consisted of only thirty men, and the prisoners knew they could overpower them, if once they could break from confinement.

The men now examined the walls and windows. The iron bars were so rusty that some of them could be moved up and down in the sockets; some could be even taken out. Then a council was held, and our lad was a prominent member. The ingenuity, endurance, and courage he had shown through all the past months set him high in the esteem of his comrades. A plan of escape was unanimously adopted. Across the entry was a huge door; a peep through the key-hole disclosed a pile of old iron. They succeeded in picking the rusty lock, and brought away such pieces as seemed serviceable. From an old iron hoop they made a murderous-looking weapon, in the shape of a sword. From other pieces they framed rude spear-heads. They tore off the bottom boards of the bunks and made rough handles for these points.

While these things were going on, two men

were stationed to watch, one at each end of the great room. If any officer approached, the signal was given in time to conceal all the preparations by throwing blankets over the pile. From time to time the prisoners drilled themselves for the desperate undertaking, each one rehearsing his part. Officers were chosen, and our little soldier became a lieutenant. In the plan of escape, he was one to lead the men who were to attack the guard. Others were to set fire to the buildings, to distract the enemy, and still another squad was to be held in reserve. The jail was built on a side-hill, and in the cellar was a great door, level with the street. This opened inward, and was fastened on the inside! From this door the men were to rush to the attack.

The time for the attempt drew near. A young artilleryman, named Martin, offered to escape alone and carry word of the plan to Arnold, who was still encamped outside the city. The signals for the army to advance to the rescue were the burning of the buildings and the firing of cannon from the gate.

But nothing could be done without powder, and for a long time no way could be devised to obtain any. At last some miniature cannon were made of paper, and the sentries were asked for a few grains of powder to charge them with. The guard at the jail was composed of good-natured, simple-

hearted Canadians, who were easily amused by the
prisoners, and deceived by Yankee wit. Un-
suspectingly they furnished a little powder now
and then, which was carefully hoarded against the
time of need. Occasionally the men made a mock
battle with their paper cannon to amuse the guards
and quiet any suspicions. Finally, some of the
simple Canadians were willing to buy powder for
the prisoners, thinking it could be used only for
innocent sport.

The money for these purchases was obtained in
a shrewd way. The good nuns in the city often
came to the jail, and gave little sums to the sick.
Looking out of the window one day, young Henry
saw a nun approaching the prison The lad's
messmate was a youth named Gibson, whose coun-
tenance was so fair and blooming as to make him
look like a blushing girl. Quick as thought the
lad told Gibson to jump into bed. He was then
covered to the chin, and the next moment the nun
came up the stairs. Henry led her to the bedside. She looked upon the bright red cheeks of
the occupant, thought he was in a high fever,
mumbled a prayer, put some money into the feebly-
extended hand, and suddenly left. She had no
sooner gone than the "sick" man was dancing
around the room with young Henry, in great glee
at the success of their little *ruse*. This money
went for powder at once.

It was now the middle of March, and the day for the outbreak was set. One difficulty only yet remained. The ice in the cellar had been gathering all winter, and the solid mass now reached above the sill of the door. Just outside the door paced a sentry, so it was impossible to pick away the ice, and it was determined that a number of men should go into the cellar on the appointed night and gently scrape away the obstruction with their pieces of rusty iron.

At last the hour had come. The prisoners had received their last drill and orders. Each man stood in the thick darkness of that upper story, grasping his rude spear or sword, nerving himself for the desperate work and waiting for the final whisper. The chosen men had gone down to clear the ice from the door. As they reached the cellar stairs they heard a slight noise below, angry shouts outside, a tumult,—and they crept hastily back to the waiting comrades and spoke three low, bitter words,—

"*We are betrayed!*"

The gloom that fell upon those hearts was heavier than the darkness of the night. But they had no time for reflection now. Enough of that by and by. They hurriedly hid their weapons beneath the bunks, under blankets, between the floors; and in a moment the tramp of men was heard upon the stairs; the guard was doubled, but the prisoners were unmolested through the night. Many were the bitter tears that fell from strong men's eyes that night. For weeks they had planned and worked, and prayed and hoped, and now all was over; liberty was but a dream.

At daylight the guards told them the story of the failure. Two young men, impatient at the delay, had gone into the cellar early in the evening, and were picking away the ice with heavy pieces of iron, when the sentry heard the noise. It was just at this moment that the men chosen for this work reached the cellar stairs. The sentry threatened to shoot through the door; then he gave the alarm, and the garrison was aroused. This account brought back a little hope to the heavy hearts. They felt that the grand plan was not discovered after all. The council met again, in the glimmering dawn, and determined to kill the one who should betray the general plot.

At sunrise came the provost and Major Murray, with a file of soldiers. The prisoners were led into the cellar and shown the futile attempt. They could truly say that they knew nothing about *that* work, and were in no way responsible for that effort to escape. Back again to the upper rooms, and after a few more questions the officers turned to go, convinced that the affair was confined to the two who had been caught. But just as hope began once more to fill every heart, a prisoner darted

H   15

through the doorway and called to the British major,—

" Sir, I have something to disclose."

It was a terrible blow. Every heart felt that this was indeed the end; every heart gave way to despair.

The traitor was led away by the guards. After a while a squad of soldiers came up the prison stairs, took the leaders in the plot, and marched them off to the governor's quarters. Sir Guy Carleton put every man under oath, and then began a searching investigation. The noble fellows would not lie; they answered every question in manly truthfulness, and claimed that they were justified in striving for their freedom. The leaders had nothing to hope. They knew the story of Ethan Allen. But their master was the kind-hearted Carleton, and not the brutal Prescott. They were sent back to the prison.

In the afternoon a file of soldiers came, with several cart-loads of chains, bilboes, and handcuffs. The prisoners in the lower rooms were ironed first, and when the upper story was reached the shackles were nearly all gone. The men were ordered to their bunks, and the officers ironed them one by one. " Never mind that lad," said the provost, as the blacksmith stepped up to Henry, and the few remaining handcuffs were placed upon the stoutest men.

No sooner had the officers left than the prisoners began upon their irons. Some had small hands, and these first slipped the cuffs. They then helped the others, and some of the irons were opened by sawing off the rivets with knife-blades notched like a saw.

So, day by day, the men cast off their irons after the morning examination, and slipped them on again before the evening rounds.

After a while the officers visited the jail three times a day, and then it became necessary for the prisoners to be constantly on the alert. They stationed watchers at each end of the long room, and great was the flurry of shackling when an officer was discovered approaching the prison.

In April the scurvy broke out in deadly manner, and made terrible havoc among the captives. Many were drawn completely out of shape, pieces of flesh dropped from their bodies, and their teeth fell out. Then came the diarrhœa, fastening upon those who had escaped the scurvy. Men died daily; the prison became a place of filth, and resounded with the groans and shrieks of the suffering. Sir Guy Carleton showed the poor prisoners much kindness. He allowed one of them to go out into the city and collect vegetable food for them, and ordered that fresh beef be given them instead of pork.

The new diet checked the ravages of scurvy, a

change in drinking-water conquered the diarrhœa, and once more the dying captives came back to life.

In May our young prisoner was astonished, and almost delighted, so selfish does suffering make one, to see his old friend, Lieutenant Simpson, come up the stairs, surrounded by a guard of soldiers. The prisoners crowded around to hear his story. It was the first word they had received from the American army outside the walls. Two ships had worked up to Quebec through the ice, bringing reinforcements to the garrison. Carleton at once prepared to attack Arnold, who was still encamped near the city. The Americans fled in haste, and Simpson, with his men, were taken by the pursuing British. The excitement of this fresh arrival had a good effect upon the despairing prisoners, and soon another happy occurrence lightened their burdens. The officers came one day to the prison accompanied by Major Carleton, a brother of the governor, who had just arrived from England. Looking upon the poor fellows, the major turned to his superiors, saying, " Ambition is laudable. Why can't these irons be taken off?" The order was given ; the blacksmith struck off the shackles, and the freed men leaped and shouted for joy. They at once got up a ball, and had a grand dance.

The men were now in rags, and the rags were

filled with vermin. The good Governor Carleton gave each one a new shirt, and the provost offered to lend our lad enough to buy a whole new suit, but the boy refused the money. He accepted, however, a small gold-piece from the officer, who showed himself anxious to relieve his sufferings. With this money the generous lad bought a few pounds of tobacco; not, however, for his own use. It was smuggled into his bunk, and one day, coming suddenly up to a group of men, he produced a large piece of the idolized weed. Their joy was indescribable. The tobacco-users had suffered tortures through all these long months, and now they fairly hugged and kissed the boy in gratitude.

, Two months more of prison-life passed on, when one morning in August brought the first approach of liberty. The provost told them that General Carleton had decided to send them to New York on parole. Soon they were led out to sign their paroles, and the kind provost-captain gave young Henry permission to walk about the city. The boy begged the favor for a few friends; it was granted, and, accompanied by an officer of the garrison, the party set out. They asked to see first the grave of their beloved Montgomery. They were taken to the spot, and the tears flowed fast as they looked upon the sad scene. Montgomery and his aides, Cheeseman and McPherson, lay side by side. The spring rains had exposed

15*

the foot of the general's coffin to the sight. The boy longed to stoop and kiss the sacred wood. With heavy hearts they turned silently away. The officer divined their natural wish, and without a word they were led to the scene of the fatal conflict. With the deepest interest they examined every detail; the attack and defense were explained, and the whole fearful struggle fought over again. Then they were led back to the jail, the locks were turned, they were prisoners once more. But the dawn of liberty soon broadened into the joyful day. It was the second week in August; the prison-doors were thrown open, the men formed in ranks, and the glorious word " Forward!" rung in every ear. What did not that word mean ? Every heart went back to the December night when in the wild storm that word came from lips now long with the dead,—when it meant—victory? Quebec? No! death and captivity. Now it spoke of freedom, home, friends, America. The men were embarked upon five transports. Our lad was placed upon the *Pearl* frigate, commanded by the brother of a boy whom he had seen saved from the scalping-knife at Point Levi. Here he had a joyful surprise. General Thompson, an old friend of his father's, had been captured a short time before at Three Rivers, and was now returning on exchange. The general had seen the lad's father in the spring, and received from him money and loving words for his wayward son, should he chance to meet him in Canada. This brought home very near. The loving words made it also seem dearer than ever. His arms stretched forth to meet his loved ones, and when, on the 10th of August, the frigate weighed anchor and spread her sails to the wind, the young soldier's heart was buoyant as the breeze that bore him on his happy way.

The struggle with the wilderness, the terrible night of death before the walls, the long months of captivity and anguish, all faded from his mind as the shores grew dim in the distance. Before him rose the pleasant home, and his mother stood in the doorway with tearful eyes and outstretched arms.

THE BEAUTIFUL SPY.

On a sultry day in the early summer of 1776, the village of Elizabethtown, New Jersey, lay almost breathless beneath the sun's fierce glare. Few signs of life were seen, for the little streets were well-nigh deserted, and in the fields the cattle crouched in the deepest shade, or stood chest-deep and motionless in the quiet streams.

The coolest spot in the village was the charming garden around the mansion of Mrs. De Hart. High above the river the great house stood, with every casement open, as if gasping for breath. A rich, glowing *parterre* stretched down the slope to the edge of a noble grove. Here the great elms and oaks lifted an impenetrable shield against the sun, and the still, cool spaces below were dreamy with the odor of wild-flowers and the cloud of perfume which floated in from the garden.

Through one of the woodland paths came a vision of startling beauty. As if the spirit of the garden had blossomed into human form, the loveliness, the grace, the aroma of flowers all met in

176

this young girl. But fourteen years of age, she had yet reached the growth and development of womanhood. Her luxuriant figure was clothed in white to the neck, where the dress fell away in fleecy folds from the still whiter throat. The rich masses of dark hair were held back from the forehead with a band of pearls, and heightened the dazzling clearness of her skin. Her eyes were brilliant and full of witchery, yet softer in light than the shady depths of the forest. Flitting down the path, her motions were graceful as the swaying of the wild-flowers that bent beneath her passing skirts. She stooped to pluck a lingering violet that looked lovingly into her face, then moved on dreamily, singing to herself in low tones of exquisite purity.

Suddenly there was a rude rustling in the woods, and a score of rough-looking men sprang out upon her, while twenty bayonets glared into her breast. The young girl clasped her hands in terror : "Oh, spare me! don't kill me! have mercy!" she cried.

The swarthy Pennsylvania riflemen hesitated, for their leader threw up his hand. They knew the girl's connection with the enemy, and had felt that she was lawful prey. But now the leader's eyes softened before her loveliness; his heart rose up against him.

"Oh, sir, you relent! Spare my life, and my father will reward you richly!"

11*

"I cannot harm you, miss," he answered, in low tones, as if speaking to himself. Then, turning sharply, he cried,—

"Come on, boys; pass her by!" And the green-coated fellows sprang quickly downward toward the river.

Released from that circle of horrid steel, the girl darted back toward the house. The young birds peeped from their nests at the beautiful vision as it sped on through the breathless woods, and along the garden-walk the flowers nodded violently after the flying form, as if wondering among themselves at the unwonted sight.

This frightened, trembling maiden, so sorely in need of a protector, was born to a wild and checkered life. She was Margaret Moncrieffe, the daughter of a British major, who was at this time an aide to Lord Cornwallis. While yet a little child, she lost the love and guidance of a noble mother, who might have altered, had she lived, the course of her wayward daughter's life. General Gage, then governor of Montreal, took the child into his family and tenderly cared for her until she was sent across the sea to Dublin and placed in a boarding-school. She did not see her father again until she was eight years old, when Major Moncrieffe was quartered in the Irish capital with his regiment. Her father was soon ordered back to America, and in 1772 he sent for his ten-year-old daughter to join

him in the new country. The major was with
General Gage in Boston, and as the war came on
Margaret was sent to Elizabethtown, to board in
the family of an American colonel. She was proud
and high-spirited, and very unhappy under the
frequent taunts of her patriot neighbors, for she
was passionately attached to her father and the
royal cause.

When Lord Howe landed at Staten Island and
besieged New York, the colonel's family fled for
safety to a town ten miles inland, taking their
young charge with them. In this dull place the
lively, volatile girl grew speedily homesick. She
had grown, in the fourteen years of her life, to
woman's estate in mind and body; she was en-
ergetic and self-reliant. When her homesickness
grew to disgust, she promptly carried out her will;
and on a Sunday, when the family were at church,
she saddled a swift horse and fled back to Elizabethtown. She went to the house of her loving
friend, Mrs. De Hart, and begged for her protection, which was kindly and generously given.

But now as her protectress held the poor girl
fluttering and sobbing in her arms, she felt that a
woman's care was not sufficient. It was evident
that Margaret's relations to the enemy had made
her an object of hatred to some of the lawless
spirits among the patriots. The British and Hessians around New York were plundering the people

and burning their dwellings.   Tales of horror came
day by day to the indignant people, and a bitter spirit
of retaliation was fast springing up in these long-
suffering hearts.   As Mrs. De Hart thought upon
Margaret's youthfulness and wonderful beauty,
upon her daring, wayward, impulsive nature, she
shrank from the great responsibility that laid upon
herself as long as the girl should remain in her
house.

It was decided that Margaret should seek the
protection of the governor of the State, who was
the brother of her father's second wife.   " Liberty
Hall," the governor's mansion, stood near the village, and thither she hastened with her hopes and
fears.

Governor Livingston was a great and good man ;
but he had a very crusty side to his nature, and
for some reason he treated the beautiful pleader
harshly.   Perhaps he was unwilling to have the
care of one who had already shown the erratic
disposition which so darkened her after-life.   Perhaps he feared to admit to his family confidence
a girl whose connections with the enemy were so
close and strong, and whose beauty might bewitch
the unwary among his numerous visitors into a
dangerous freedom of speech concerning the patriots' designs.   However it may have been, the
governor turned her away ; and if the latter reason
was indeed the one that moved him, he must have

reflected with pleasure, as events rolled on, upon the shrewdness of his discernment.

Disappointed, Margaret went back to her good protectress, with her fears turned to certainty and her hopes to bitterness. The tender soul of her loving friend was now in great perplexity. What could *she* do with the girl, when one so nearly allied to her was afraid to throw around her the protection of his name?

But Margaret, quick, impulsive, daring, conceived a bold scheme, and immediately set it in motion. She had often heard of General Putnam, the kind, bluff, soft-hearted Yankee general, and she determined to make an appeal to him.

A few days after this decision, General Putnam received, at his quarters in New York, a letter addressed to himself in the daintiest of feminine hands, and whose folds breathed the delicate odor of violets that carried him back to his boyhood among the Connecticut hills. With much curiosity the old warrior opened the missive as tenderly as if he were unswathing a new-born child. Its contents filled him with astonishment. From the daughter of Major Moncrieffe, his comrade in many a weary march and fiery battle through the old French war, but now, alas, his enemy! And claiming *his* fatherly protection, too! For the letter told the whole story of the writer's situation,—her danger, her fears, her need of a protector whose age and position should throw a mantle around her good name as well as shield her from rude hostility.

The kind, rough, tender heart of the glorious old wolf-fighter was touched. He took the letter, in which the tears of his comrade's daughter mingled with the wild-flowers' perfume, and laid it before his wife and daughters.

"My 'protection'?" cried the good man; "certainly she shall have it, at once!"

And this is the answer which the waiting, hoping, trembling Margaret received,—

"I have, agreeably to your desire, waited on his Excellency, to endeavor to obtain permission for you to go to Staten Island. As the Congress have reserved to themselves the right of exchanging prisoners, the general has sent to know their pleasure, and doubts not they will give their consent. . . . If agreeable to you, be assured, miss, you shall be sincerely welcome. You will here, I think, be in a more probable way of accomplishing the end you wish,—that of seeing your father,—and may depend upon every civility from, miss, your obedient servant,

"ISRAEL PUTNAM."

The next day, Colonel Webb, an aide to General Putnam, came out to Elizabethtown to escort the young girl into the city.

When Margaret reached headquarters, on Broad-
way, Mrs. Putnam and her daughters greeted her
with the utmost tenderness. They were charmed
with the loveliness and vivacity of the young girl,
who speedily won her way to their hearts. On
the day after her arrival, Margaret was presented
to General Washington and his wife. These two
noble souls also felt great sympathy with the lonely
maiden in her peculiar situation, and constantly
showed her the kindest attentions.

Margaret now entered upon a new life. The
homely New England ways of the general's family
afforded her much amusement, though they were
hardly to her taste. The gay society to which she
had long been accustomed was entirely wanting in
her new home. The sternness of war was round
about her on every side. Recreations were few;
every one was filled with the spirit of work. Mrs.
Putnam was famous for her spinning, and the
dainty hands of the beautiful stranger were kept
at work upon the flax, while her feet found more
exercise in turning the wheel than in dancing. The
fingers that were so skillful with the harp and the
brush did not take very kindly to the prosaic spinning-wheel; but the American soldiers needed
shirts, and the low, droning hum became far more
intimate with the shapely little ears than the melo-
dies of the masters of song. Margaret's beautiful
needlework also was often sought for by the kind

old general, towards whom her impressive heart
went out in sincere respect and gratitude.

Kind as her new friends were, they did not forget
that she was the daughter of a British officer, and
in full sympathy with the royal cause.   Her facili-
ties for getting information of the patriots' designs
were numerous, and so a strict watch was kept
upon her movements, and she was seldom allowed
to be alone.   There was, however, one place of
retirement which she enjoyed unmolested.   Like
many of the dwellings in the city at that time, the
residence of the general officers had an open gal-
lery on the roof, which commanded a broad view
of the country and the bay.   Here Margaret spent
many quiet hours, viewing through a telescope the
British camps and the British fleet in the harbor.
Her father was stationed with Lord Percy on Staten
Island, and thither her longing eyes the oftenest
turned.   Her heart flew far away to those gleaming
lines of tents, but she felt it was vain to wish, for
she recognized the fact that she was looked upon
as a sort of prisoner of state, whom her hosts were
at present unwilling to relinquish.

Her situation was sometimes embarrassing and
painful.   Often a well-meant jest brought her great
annoyance, which was increased by her impulsive-
ness or the failure of her usually ready wit.

At the dinner-table one day, the toast was "The
Congress."   The loyal-hearted British maiden did

not drink her wine. General Washington noticed
the omission, and said, with a touch of sarcasm in
his tone,—

"Miss Moncrieffe, you do not drink."

Margaret blushed at this rebuke, and lost her
presence of mind. Lifting her glass, she suddenly
said,—

"General Howe is the toast," and drank with
a hearty relish. This daring speech was like a
bombshell in the midst of the company. They
began to reprove her sharply, when General Putnam came gallantly to her rescue.

"I am sure," said the kind old soldier, "that the
lass did not mean to offend. Besides, everything
said or done by such a child ought to amuse, and
not affront you."

The poor girl turned beaming eyes of gratitude
upon her defender, and General Washington said
to her, in his dignified way,—

"Well, miss, I will overlook your indiscretion
on condition that you drink my health or General
Putnam's the first time you dine at Sir William
Howe's table, on the other side of the water."

Margaret's heart bounded at these words. She
thought she would now be released. She clapped
her hands in outburst of joy and longing, and
promised the chief to do anything he wished if
only he would send her to her father. But her
hopes were soon dispelled. Her girlish enthusiasm

was coldly met, while her very eagerness to be free caused her to be more closely watched than ever.

Within a few days of this unfortunate dinner, a party of British officers came to the American headquarters, bearing a flag of truce and a demand for his daughter from Major Moncrieffe. Washington refused to deliver the girl. Her tears and pleadings were in vain. From this day she looked upon the commander with aversion. She felt that her captivity was cruel, and that she was kept a hostage for her father's good behavior. But the wise chief had his own good reasons for all he did, and an incident which had just occurred made him very suspicious of his beautiful prisoner.

The brilliant young Aaron Burr, a mere lad in years, but already an experienced soldier, was at this time an aide to General Putnam, and a member of his family.

Fresh from the glory of that terrible expedition to Quebec, handsome, fascinating, dashing, he was a favorite in the American camp. Lovely, lively, accomplished, Margaret Moncrieffe was very attractive to the young brigade-major, who enjoyed her vivacity, her exquisite singing, and her keen wit. Yet he never forgot her peculiar situation, and was very watchful of her movements.

One day he found her at her favorite amusement of painting. He stood behind her seat and watched the beautiful flowers grow under her touch. Soon his quick, keen eye detected some strange-looking lines painted lightly among the flowers. He followed them as they zigzagged in and out, and was astonished to discover the plan of an important fort hidden in this cluster of roses. The young aide hastened to his general, and disclosed the devices of the beautiful spy. It was determined to remove her from headquarters to a more secluded place, where she could be more closely watched. She was at once sent a few miles inland, to Kingsbridge, and placed in the hands of General Mifflin.

The general's wife was a Quaker lady, beautiful, accomplished, and very lovely in disposition. She showed a motherly tenderness to Margaret, and was gradually winning a sweet, healthful influence over her. But suddenly the wayward maiden fell in love! Young Major Burr was a frequent visitor to Kingsbridge, and Margaret's impressible heart followed all his coming and going. Her impulsive nature, once aroused, could not easily be controlled; all the quiet peace of her new life was gone.

She now wrote to General Putnam, and confided to him all her feelings. Her good old friend was greatly troubled at this turn of affairs. In his blunt, true-hearted way he tried to wean her from the new love. He showed her the bitter enmity existing between her father and Major Burr, and

made her tremble as he pictured her lover drenching his sword in her father's blood should they
chance to meet in battle.

The poor girl was in deep distress; she had
given away her heart and she was powerless to
take it back. Yet she was devotedly attached to
her father and her king.

The young brigade-major now came less frequently to Kingsbridge, and whenever General
Putnam visited her, he appeared troubled in her
presence, watched her keenly, and was extremely
reserved. Meanwhile, he laid her case before the
Continental Congress, and strove in every way to
be relieved of a care which weighed heavily upon
his heart. At length Congress gave him permission to send the troublesome maiden to her father.

Her joy at her coming release was strongly
mixed with pain. She felt, as she afterwards said,
that she was turning her back on liberty. The end
proved that this was indeed the greatest turning-
point in her life. The sweet influences among
which she had dwelt might have led her into a
noble and happy womanhood; but she was sent
forth into the reckless dissipation of the British
camp, and her young life soon passed into the
cloud of a cruel marriage.

The kind-hearted Putnam determined to honor
his grateful charge by returning her to Major Moncrieffe with a noble escort. The barge of the

Continental Congress was ordered to convey her down New York Bay to the British fleet, and General Knox, with his staff, formed her escort of honor.

The rough wind tossed the great barge about like an egg-shell, and drenched the frightened girl with the salt water. The American officers showed her the utmost courtesy, but Margaret was wretched at heart, and their kind efforts called out no response,—all her vivacity had vanished.

As the party drew near to the *Eagle* man-of-war, the flag-ship of Lord Howe, a British officer bearing a flag of truce entered the admiral's barge and swiftly approached. General Knox had been ordered to deliver his charge at headquarters, but the British officer told him that this was impossible, as no person from the American lines was allowed to approach nearer the English fleet. Margaret stepped aboard the British barge and was taken to the man-of-war. From Lord Howe's ship it was but a short distance to the camp on Staten Island, and Margaret's name was soon announced at headquarters.

The commander-in-chief, Sir William Howe, sent an aide to invite the new-comer to his table, as she had arrived at the dinner-hour. Margaret had not a moment to arrange her disordered appearance. With wind-blown hair, flushed cheeks, and eyes brilliant from excitement, she was led to the table where sat the chief surrounded with his gallant suite.

Her wonderful beauty was heightened by her embarrassment, and her romantic history was known to all the officers; they vied with one another to do her honor. She was seated beside the wife of Major Montresor, who had been her friend from childhood, and her bright spirits soon returned under the merry influences of the hour. The pleasure-loving British commander was a famous feaster, and the wit flew rapidly around the table. He turned at last to beautiful Margaret Moncrieffe, and called upon her for a toast.

"General Putnam!" she cried.

"Oh," said Colonel Sheriff, "you must not give him here!"

"By all means," replied Sir William Howe, with his kindest smile,—"by all means; if he be the lady's sweetheart I can have no objection to drink his health."

The laughter of the company threw the girl into a blushing embarrassment. Impulsively she handed to Sir William a letter which General Putnam had sent by her to the British commander. She was now told that her father was stationed with Lord Percy. Her desire to find him at once was very strong. The courteous Sir William gave her his carriage, and from all the officers who were eager to escort so charming a girl she chose Colonel

Small, whom she had known from childhood. A drive of nine miles through a charming country brought Margaret to Lord Percy's headquarters. The earl and Major Moncrieffe were pacing the lawn. With a cry of delight Margaret sprang into her father's arms. Lord Percy at once gave up one of his own apartments to the beautiful guest, and here she stayed until the British army left the island.

When the royal troops took possession of New York, Major Moncrieffe recovered his property in the city. His son had been adopted by Lord Cornwallis, but Margaret remained with her father, who now moved into his own house, to which he invited the widow of a British officer as companion for his daughter. Here she speedily became a queen in society. Her marvelous beauty drew all hearts to herself, while her accomplishments, her brilliancy, and her loveliness of disposition kept all the hearts she gained. Many were the officers who strove to win her love, but she treated them all with equal favor,—one among the enemy had already conquered her heart.

Her triumphant reign, however, was soon broken by a new romance in her strange young life.

On the banks of the Hudson River there lived, about seven miles from Peekskill, a wealthy American patriot, whose name was Wood. His wife, however, was an Englishwoman, whose early asso-

ciations made her long for more lively society than
she could find among her republican neighbors.
She was related to Major Moncrieffe, and she now
invited his daughter to visit her lovely home.
Margaret came, accompanied by a maid-servant,
and trunks enough for a royal traveler.

There were three daughters in the family, and
a little son twelve years of age. With music and
games, and with rides among the grand hills of the
Hudson, the days flew joyously on. The simple
country-folk gazed with wonder on the grace and
beauty of the elegant young lady, and they were
dazzled by the splendor of her attire and adorn-
ments. Her wardrobe was so extensive that her
chamber could not contain all her garments.

Margaret was especially fond of riding, and she
was as graceful in the saddle as on her feet. Her
horse was a beast of high mettle, and in perfect
sympathy with his dashing rider. It was a sight
for the plain farming people to enjoy, when this
graceful pair sped wildly by to and from the hills.
The men looked up from the ground and leaned
upon their hoes to gaze after the flying vision,
while the good housewives and farm-lassies left
all their work and rushed to the doors when they
heard the wild clatter approaching. The simple-
mannered women cared more for a glimpse of the
dress than of the wearer. The richness of Margaret's array was like a vision of the Arabian Nights

to these homespun dwellers among the river-hills. Her riding-habit was a sight worth running to see. The cloth was a rich, deep blue. The long skirt hung in heavy folds from a jacket that fitted closely to her magnificent figure. The jacket was trimmed with gold lace and thrown open in front, disclosing a buff vest studded with buttons of the finest gold. This vest, also, fell open toward the throat, and displayed a shirt bosom of the whitest linen and the finest ruffles, while her throat was covered with a white lawn neckhandkerchief edged with lace.

Ere long every child in the neighborhood knew the lady who was as kind as she was beautiful. Mr. Wood's home was crowded with visitors, eager to see and know the lovely stranger. Her manners were courtly and winning, her voice marvelously soft and sweet, while her eyes held every one in chains. Pleased with their homage, she would sing and play for their delight, and even allow them to watch her at painting or drawing.

She was now within the American lines, and many were the young patriot officers who came under the power of her witchery, flocking about her like moths around a glowing light. She fascinated them not only by her loveliness, but by the deep interest she showed in the cause for which they were fighting. Born in America and connected with some of the most famous patriot families, she pretended to be at heart a sympathizer with her new friends and adorers. The young officers were charmed into a fatal confidence in their beautiful enemy; they poured into her ears the secrets of the camp and council. So this wonderful girl of fourteen became a British spy.

One bright, glorious morning late in the year the hoof-beats of Margaret's fiery horse rang out upon the frosty air. It was somewhat earlier than her accustomed hour, and no one was upon the road. But the horses neighed shrilly from the barns as she clattered by, and half-dressed forms peered curiously from the curtained windows to catch a glimpse of the famous beauty.

She was the very picture of innocence. Her sunny face glowed with the delight of the morning, and she seemed to be the spirit of sunrise bursting upon the sleeping hamlets. Yet, under that artfully-artless face a deceitful heart was scheming evil; even now she was on an errand of treason. A keen dash of a few miles brought in sight a heavy clump of trees,—the goal of her ride. Once having passed this, she could turn about and jog homeward at her leisure. A nervous flutter seized her as she drew near. Often before had she come hither on the same mission, but now she felt as if pursued. Instinctively she plied her riding-whip; the mettle-some beast tossed his foaming nostrils in the air and sprang on with furious energy. Suddenly a dog rushed out from a farm-yard with loud barks; the horse took fright, shied, and threw his rider.

The women in the farm-house flew to the rescue. They found the young girl unconscious. They lifted her and carried her tenderly in. They dashed water into the blanched face; they chafed the hands and feet; one of them unbuttoned the gorgeous vest. As the vest flew open a sealed letter fell upon the floor. The simple-hearted woman picked it up and laid it on the table, merely thinking, as she looked on the face just flushing with the return of consciousness, " It is no wonder she has a lover."

Just as the farmer himself came into the room Margaret faintly opened her eyes. Seeing her vest thrown back, she leaped suddenly up and with clasped hands cried in piteous tones, " Who opened my waistcoat? Where is the letter? I am ruined! Oh, I am lost, lost!"

The unsuspecting woman hastened to give the letter to the weeping girl, but the farmer sprang forward and seized it,—his suspicions were aroused. He looked at the address: it was to a British officer in New York. Margaret watched his face through her tears; again she broke into pleading; she begged piteously for the letter; she assured him it was only to a lover; she tried all her powers of charming; she offered rich rewards if he would give it up. But the honest man's purpose was only strengthened by these wild demonstrations. He walked away with the letter.

Margaret was uninjured by her fall, with the exception of a few slight bruises. Her horse had been caught, and now stood in the yard. The girl hastily gathered up her long skirt, passed out of the house with a few agitated words of thanks to the wondering women, mounted her steed, and dashed off toward the home of her friends.

Meanwhile, the man who had awaited her coming in the woods, a young American lieutenant, having witnessed the accident, waited fearfully for Margaret's reappearance, and now, as she turned her back upon him in flight, felt that they were betrayed, and hurried away in another direction.

Arriving at the house, Margaret confided all to her hostess. No time was to be lost; capture would be speedy, and spies, when caught, were— hung! Aided by her maid and by Mrs. Wood, the daring girl who had been playing so dangerous a game hastily collected her wardrobe for immediate flight to New York. But now the wealth which had been her pride became her ruin. Before all things could be packed a squad of American soldiers had surrounded the house. An officer entered and demanded Miss Margaret Moncrieffe. She was forced to finish her packing, as all her baggage was wanted also. She was then taken to a tavern among the hills, and a guard was placed over her. Her baggage was sent to headquarters. The letter which had betrayed her had been opened, and found to contain important information for the British commander in New York. Her trunks were now examined. Many valuable papers were found, and it was evident that this person, although scarcely out of childhood, had been a very successful spy.

The excitement in camp increased when Lieutenant Newman came forward and confessed that he had been implicated with the girl. It seems she had been accustomed to write down the information she obtained from time to time, and on the appointed days she would ride past the clump of woods, where the lieutenant would be concealed, and drop the letter in the road for him to pick up. He then passed it to another traitor down the river, and thus it reached New York. The young officer had been completely bewitched by the artful beauty, and now was deeply penitent. He had a family in the vicinity, and pleaded piteously to be spared. He was arrested and kept, at present, under heavy guards.

From the tavern windows across the Hudson Margaret could see the friendly home from which she had been so suddenly torn. It looked so peaceful, nestling there among the hills. How many joyous hours she had spent within those walls! And what would be the end? She looked into the poor bit of glass that adorned her bare room, and, seeing her beautiful white throat, shuddered as she thought of the fate of spies.

Day after day went by. Her guards, at first glum and even harsh, gradually melted before her beauty and winning ways; she was allowed to walk out, but always accompanied by an officer. They were anxious days to her, for she was ignorant of her fate.

Meanwhile, the British officers made constant appeals to the American commander. They pleaded the maiden's youthfulness, her high social position, and the brilliant promise of her life.

It had been determined that she should be tried as a spy, but the hearts of the patriots were tender, and at last they released her from bondage. She was taken down the river and given into the hands of her friends, who had come out from the city to receive her.

She was restored unharmed to her father with the simple condition that she should never again be found within the American lines.

THE ANGEL OF THE HOUSE.

THE beautiful month of October, 1776, brought little harvest joy to the dwellers on the western end of Long Island.

All over that lovely country, far and near, were pitched the camps of the British and Hessian soldiers; the great farm-houses were filled with officers, who had quartered themselves on the inhabitants; the village shops were noisy with a drunken and quarrelsome rabble, and no one who was friendly to the American cause was safe from insult and injury.

Nearly all the patriots were away from their homes, fighting in Washington's army; but a few still remained, kept back by old age or weakness. Other men stayed on their pleasant farms, but for far different reasons. These were Tories, who took sides with the king, and, while they enjoyed the comforts of their own homes, were bitter in their enmity to their patriotic neighbors.

Led by these men, the foreign soldiers trampled the rich harvests under the feet of their chargers, plundered the barns and granaries, seized the horses, drove off the cattle to their camps, and robbed the houses of all that was worth carrying away. Worse than all this, sometimes, when the frightened women and children sat crying by the desolate hearth, these soldiers lighted the torch and burned their houses over their heads.

Many were the tales of horror told beside the autumn fire or around the evening lamp; and the coming of night, which should have brought rest and quiet, brought only a longing for the morning light.

One of these October evenings settled down with unusual peacefulness upon the farm which is the scene of our story. No new events had happened during the day, and the cattle had gone to their stalls, the hens to their roosts, with calmer feelings than usual. Now and then a slight sound of uneasiness might be heard among the hens, dreaming, perhaps, of red-coats, high boots, and fierce bayonets; for had they not seen their neighbors over the way carried off by the feet or raised aloft on the points of English steel?

In-doors, near the great log-fire, sat pussy, who was the only domestic creature unmoved by the scenes of violence around her from day to day. Being good neither for the table nor the harness, the family cat always escaped the destruction when it broke over the head of her master.

Around the table were gathered a still unbroken

family. With lighter hearts than usual the little ones were playing about, while the older people talked in low tones of the war, the sad scenes of the past weeks, the sufferings of their neighbors, and the hopes of peace. By and by the little prayers were said at mother's knee, the father thanked God that they had thus far been kept from harm, and the children were getting ready for bed.

Suddenly a heavy *thud*, as of something sharp plunged into the outer door, and, quivering after the blow, hushed every voice and filled the eyes with fear. Little feet fled to mother's side in terror, while the father, weak with sickness, rose to unlatch the door. The impatient scuffling and murmuring without told plainly what the danger was that now glared at the dear old home. But there were no means of defense, and perhaps a kind "welcome" might disarm hostility.

The farmer opened the door,—but no welcome was waited for. A huge, red-coated officer snatched his sword from the door, into which he had driven it, and, followed by a dozen drunken soldiers, thrust the old man aside and pressed into the house. With fierce threats they demanded money, plate, jewels,—everything valuable.

" You can find nothing of that kind here," said the farmer; "I am not rich. But pray be gentle, and we will entertain you as well as we can."

To this soft answer they replied with rude threats

unless money was at once given them. The children peeped out from their mother's gown, curious,
in the midst of their fear, to see the bright uniforms. But there was no pleasant look in any
man's face, and the ugly-looking swords frightened
them; they shrank back, shivering, and covered
their faces with mother's skirts.

The rough men swung their swords over the
parents' heads, threatening instant death. But no
money was forthcoming, and with wild shouts the
soldiers rushed from room to room, spreading
themselves all through the house, and began a
ruthless search.

There were many valuables in the house,—coins
of gold and silver, plate and family jewels,—heir-
looms brought here by their ancestors from the
low shores of Holland,—rich silks and velvets
which had been worn at weddings and funerals, on
all great occasions, for more than a century.

But when the Hessians were first quartered in
the neighborhood, the prudent farmer stowed his
wealth into a little blind room which opened from
the sitting-room; the door was then covered, and
a great cupboard moved against it; so it was entirely hidden.

The soldiers burst open trunks and chests; they
ransacked closets and drawers; they scattered
everything in dreadful confusion. The father remonstrated, the mother pleaded, but whatever the

men fancied they seized, and the rest they broke in pieces, tore in shreds, and ruined. Pussy jumped on to the great clock in the corner, and crouched, glowering upon them in fear and rage. The noise spread to the farm-yards and barns, where the lowing of the cattle and complainings of the fowls showed their fear at the unusual disturbance. The children followed their parents from room to room, clinging to their skirts and crying with grief and fright. Little dresses were torn from neck to hem, cherished toys were trampled under the heavy boots, stockings and flannels thrust into pockets and pouches; and when the soldiers had stolen all they wanted, they amused themselves by driving their bayonets through the windows and hurling chairs at the mirrors.

Half a dozen men had found their way at last into the nursery, and their coarse shouts of laughter told of the sport they were enjoying. At once the children forgot their terror; they flew to the baby-house, and with kicks, screams, and scratchings they fought desperately in defense of their dolls.

The men only laughed the louder. They crushed the baby furniture and crockery, and, sticking their bayonets into the captured dolls, waved them over their heads, thrust them into the children's faces, and shouted with glee at their attempts at rescue.

Little Katrine, but four years old, snatched her favorite Bess, and, running into the closet, hid away beneath the heap of clothes.

But all the other dolls were in the hands of the enemy. The victory had been complete, and the once happy home of the pets was desolate and in ruins.

Little did the dolls think, when they were kissed and laid away tenderly for the night, that the fortunes of war were so soon to be theirs!

Meanwhile, the farmer had not ceased to remonstrate, and to threaten to tell his story to the commanding officer of the camp, till the soldiers, enraged at finding no money, swore they would burn the house at once. Going into the kitchen, they seized flaming brands from the hearth, and, rushing into the open air, set a lighted torch at each corner of the house. The terrified family followed the ruffians with tears and pleadings, and now stood grouped before their doomed dwelling in grief and terror.

Only Sarah, the eldest daughter, was not there. A noble-looking girl of sixteen, she had kept out of sight as much as possible, fearing that her beauty might put her in danger. Now, at this terrible moment, she came flying down the steps, her arms extended in pleading, her loosened hair streaming in the wind, her cheeks and beautiful eyes aglow with intense excitement.

She stopped in front of the officer. Famed through all the north country for her loveliness, she really looked now like a heavenly apparition. He gazed upon her as in a trance; the lighted torch drooped in his hand,—he stood in awe before the purity of her presence. Who knows but at that moment, out of the darkness of the night, some sweet child-face from his home beyond the sea looked tenderly into his eyes and softened his heart to a father's love?

At length he spoke:

"Angel!"

"Oh, spare us!" cried Sarah, with clasped hands.

"I will, on one condition," said the officer, standing motionless, with eyes full of admiration.

"What is that?"

"Will you grant it?"

"Yes, if I can," she replied, with almost a tremble.

"Then," said the man, "will you let me kiss you just once?"

With half-frightened eyes Sarah turned to her father, to read his thought.

"If that is all," said the old man, with softened voice, "comply at once, my daughter."

So the great rough soldier stepped forward, dropping his torch, and treading out the flame in his eagerness; his high grenadier bearskin cap brushed her bright hair, and he pressed a hearty kiss upon her pure mouth. Then, immediately turning to his men, he called them off, and departed.

It was a strange scene,—the tall officer, now sobered and thoughtful, walking slowly down the lane, the men following in disorder and noisy amazement, every bayonet bearing a doll on its point—some in full costume and some in night-dress, as they were laid away; while the smouldering torches cast gigantic shadows into the trees, and the rescued dwelling stood sombre and still in the darkness.

As the pure-hearted maiden kneeled beside her bed that night, who can doubt that she thanked her Father in heaven, perhaps for the first time, for the beauty which had saved her loved ones from destruction? While, in a neighboring chamber, her earthly father blessed the good God of mercy for sending them, that night, the Angel of His Presence!

THE DOVE'S NEST IN THE LION'S DEN.

In 1776 the western end of Long Island was overrun with the English troops and mercenaries. There was no security to life or property; everything was at the mercy of the wicked Hessians.

At this time there was living on the island, and not far from New York, a Quaker family by the name of Pattison. Henry Pattison, the father, was one of the strictest of the sect; of a noble, generous nature, a kind neighbor, and a wise counselor. He was universally loved and revered. He won the name of The Peace-Maker.

He owned a fine farm, and was growing wealthy, when the war came, and sad days settled down upon the community. Mother Pattison was the true type of the Quaker wife and mother. Under her tidy white cap beamed the placid, tender face which is so common among these pure-hearted people, and her skillful advice and winning words of consolation were often heard in the house of the sick and afflicted. Eight sturdy boys and one little sweet, timid flower of a daughter blessed this good couple, and made their home one of happiness and love.

Edmund, the oldest son, was a handsome, manly lad of eighteen. Beneath his broad-brimmed hat, his quiet "thee" and "thou," beat a fiery and fearless heart that often broke through the mild Quaker training, and made him, notwithstanding his peace principles, a leader among his fellows.

One day as he sat in the barn, quietly enjoying his noonday rest, a British trooper rode up to the door. Seeing Edmund, he shouted,—

"Come, youngster, make haste and stir yourself! Go and help my driver there unload that cart of timber into the road!"

Now Edmund had just been loading that wood 'to carry it to a neighbor to whom it belonged. Both wagon and oxen belonged to his father.

"Come, hurry!" said the horseman.

"I shall not do it!" said Edmund.

"What,—sirrah!" cried the ruffian, "we shall see who will do it!" And he flourished his sword over the boy's head, swearing and threatening to cut him down unless he instantly obeyed. Edmund stood unflinchingly, fiercely eying the enraged soldier.

Just then a little boy, Charles, the son of a neighbor, ran into the house and told Mrs. Pattison that "a Britisher was going to kill her Edmund." She rushed to the barn, begged the soldier to stop, and pleaded with her son to unload the wood and so save his life.

"No fear of death, mother; he dare not touch a hair of my head."

"Dare not?" cried the horseman, as he swung his sword before the lad's face, and swore he would kill him instantly.

"You dare not!" said Edmund, firmly; "and I will report you to your master for this."

The fierce, defiant look really awed the trooper, and he mounted his horse, although he still told the boy he would "cut him into inch pieces."

Edmund knew that such things were actually done by the soldiers, and he appreciated the man's terrible rage. He coolly walked across the barn-floor and armed himself with a pitchfork.

"You cowardly rascal!"—the boy's words came fierce and sharp: "now take one step towards this floor and I stab you with my pitchfork."

The gentle Mrs. Pattison expected to see her boy at once shot down like a dog. She ran to the house, and, meeting her husband, sent him to the rescue.

Friend Pattison rode hastily up, and said calmly to the trooper, "You have no right to lay a finger on that boy, who is a non-combatant."

The man did not move.

Then Farmer Pattison turned toward the road,

saying he would ride and call Colonel Wurms, who commanded the troops.

Upon this the horseman, thinking it best for *him* to see his master first, drove the spurs into his horse and galloped away, uttering vows of vengeance.

The little boy who had alarmed Mrs. Pattison was a lad of fourteen, the son of a neighbor who was in Washington's army.

Sitting one day under the trees with the little Pattisons, talking indignantly of the " British thieves," he saw a light-horseman ride up toward a farm-house just across the pond. He guessed at once what the man was after. He tried to signal the farmer, but in vain.

" They are pressing horses!" cried Charlie; " they always ride that way when stealing horses."

He thought of his father's beautiful colt,—his own pet.

" Fleetwood shall not go!" said he. Running as fast as he could to the barn, he leaped on the colt's back and started for the woods.

The red-coat saw him, and, putting spurs to his horse, rising in the saddle and shouting, he tore down the road at headlong speed.

Charlie's mother rushed to the door. She saw her little son galloping towards the woods with his murderous enemy close upon his heels. Her heart beat fearfully, and she gave one great cry of prayer as her brave boy dashed into the thick woods and out of sight, still hotly pursued by the soldier.

The trees were close-set and the branches low. Charlie laid down along the colt's neck to escape being swept off. He cheered on, with low cries, the wild colt, who stretched himself full length at every leap.

With streaming mane, glaring eyes, distended nostrils, he plunged onward. Charlie heard the dead, dry boughs crackling behind him, and the snorting of the soldier's horse, so near was his fierce pursuer. On, on, Fleetwood dashed, bearing his little master from one piece of woods to another, till the forest became dense and dark. He had now gained some on the soldier; and, seeing ahead a tangled, marshy thicket, Charlie rode right into its midst. Here he stood five hours without moving.

The soldier, so much heavier with his horse, dared not venture into the swamp. He rode round and round, seeking for some firm spot of entrance. Sometimes he did come very near; but every time sinking into the wet, springy bog, he was obliged to give it up; he could not even get a shot at the boy, the brush was so thick, and Fleetwood instinctively still as a mouse; and, finally, with loud oaths, he rode off.

The lad and the colt still stood there, hour

after hour, not knowing whether they might venture out; but at nightfall his mother, who had been watching all the while, with tears and prayers, saw her dear boy cautiously peeping through the edge of the woods. By signs she let him know that the danger was past, and, riding up to the house, he dismounted. Then, leaning against his beautiful colt, his own bright, golden curls mingling with Fleetwood's ebon mane, the plucky little fellow told his adventures to the eager group.

The Quaker neighbors in this vicinity had at last been driven, by the outrages of the hostile troops, to use some means of defense. They agreed that whenever a house should be attacked the family would fire a gun, which would be answered by firing from the other houses, and so the neighborhood become alarmed.

But Farmer Pattison so abhorred the use of a gun that he would have none in his house. He procured a conch-shell, which, when well blown, could be heard a great way.

One night, while Charlie's family were all soundly sleeping, and without the clear November air was unstirred by a breath of wind, suddenly the grum report of the conch boomed in at the windows and alarmed the whole house.

Wakened so unceremoniously, all thought it was a gun; but no one could tell whence it came. The venerable grandfather knelt in prayer; the sick

English officer staying at the house ordered his two guards to prepare for defense; the mother sat trembling, while the two little girls, Grace and Marcia, hid their faces in their mother's night-dress.

But our Charlie was brave. He loaded the old fire-arm, and, going down to the piazza, blazed away, loading and firing, to frighten away the unseen foe. •Through the still air could be heard the guns of the neighbors, all aroused to defend their homes.

But no burning building could be seen, nor were there any shouts or noises of conflict.

The alarm subsided; but for the rest of the night the little family sat anxious and waited for the dawn. In the morning they learned the cause of the alarm. It seems that at noon, the day before, the Pattison boys were trying their lungs on the conch, calling the hired men to dinner. Little Joseph stood by, waiting his turn, but it did not come. Dinner was ready, and the shell was put away on the shelf over the kitchen-door. The little fellow's disappointment was great, and that night he dreamed of robbers, of English soldiers and burning houses. He dreamed that he must blow the shell.

Up he jumped, ran down-stairs, and through two rooms, still asleep, and, standing in a chair, got the conch from the shelf. Going to the back door, he blew it lustily and aroused the whole family. They rushed down-stairs in great alarm, and there stood the little boy bareheaded and in his night-gown, while great drops of perspiration stood on his face.

The light and joy of Farmer Pattison's house was the sweet little daughter Edith. She was the dearest little Quakeress. Her hair and eyes were quite dark, but her face was pure and fair, her expression mild and gentle, and in all her ways she was modest and winning. She usually wore a silvery-drab poplin; the sleeves came just above the dimpled elbows, with a little white frill below, showing her soft arms, round and white. She wore always a neat gauze cap, for the Quakers thought it unseemly that a young woman's head should be uncovered. It is very easy to describe Edith's outward appearance, but words cannot paint the spiritual expression of her sweet face or the charm of her heart.

Her eight brothers made a perfect queen of her, and it was beautiful to see the great, sturdy boys fetch and carry for her, and obey her slightest wish.

Of course this little gem could not be hidden, however plain was the setting, and Edith was everywhere known and worshiped. Plow-boys and farmers' sons, common soldiers and officers, all felt the influence of her pure face and tender eyes.

Many were the marked attentions which the

little Quakeress received, but her unconscious
heart took them all with charming innocence, and
lived on undisturbed by any dreams of love.

This could not always last. Among the English
officers stationed in the neighborhood was one of
a very different sort from most of his comrades.

Captain Morton was a noble-looking man, young,
handsome, and dashing, with a heart possessed of
many fine qualities. He was a frequent visitor at
the Pattisons' and had become enslaved by the
gentleness and charm of the young Quakeress,
who was for a long time unconscious of what she
had done. They could often be seen walking together, and a beautiful sight it was,—she in her
demure mien, little close bonnet, and sober, gray
dress; he by her side, with proud step, clad in
scarlet and gold, and his bright plume bending
low to her face.

At length he began to plead with her, but she,
half frightened, gently repulsed him. The soldier's
profession was wholly repugnant to her. Above
the fife and drum she heard the groans of the
wounded, the cry of the dying,—and the wail of
widows and orphans filled her heart.

Meeting with so little favor, Captain Morton
kept away from Edith for many weeks. At last,
driven to despair, he entered the house suddenly
one day and stood before the maiden. She was
sitting at the spinning-wheel, and the low, quiet

music was well in tune with the gentle and happy thoughts that filled her mind. Her graceful figure and serene face were always seen to advantage while she turned the wheel with light step and held the slender thread in her shapely fingers.

Edith was now grieved to see the officer. She thought he had gone from the neighborhood. He began to speak very abruptly.

"Edith, you have not seen me for some time, in accordance with your wish; I have been trying my self-control. Look at me! Behold my success!"

She turned her eyes to his face, and was astonished at the change in his appearance.

"Give me hope," he cried, "or I die; some word of comfort, a look of love, some promise for my thoughts to feed on in my absence. To-morrow, with this precious boon, I go; without it, this is my resource."

So saying, the desperate lover drew his pistol and pointed it at his breast. Edith was terrified, but, with her natural quietness of manner, she left her wheel, and gently but firmly took the pistol from his hand and laid it aside.

"The intemperance thou showest," said Edith, her quiet eyes looking steadfastly at his, "would intimidate me from forming any closer intimacy with thee. And how dost thou think it would seem to the Friends, if I should form an engagement with one who lifts up his sword against his fellow-men ?"

" Do not set that down against me," pleaded the officer. "Am I to blame for being bred a soldier, for being an instrument to suppress rebellion ? The Friends are generally supposed to be on our side."

" I know," said Edith, "they are called Tories, but unjustly, for they espouse neither cause. They are opposed to the war."

" But you, Edith, surely want to see the rebellion crushed !"

" Nay," answered she; " I fervently wish for peace ; but you have oppressed us wrongfully, and domineered over us until patience hath had her perfect work and seemeth no longer to be a virtue. And I venture to predict that the side which is led by so good a man as George Washington will be successful."

The captain was greatly surprised at this outbreak, and disappointed also. However, his love conquered his resentment, and he promised to think soberly of all she had said.

He had been mistaken in her feelings towards him,—she had really begun to love him. His hopes now seemed to rise. He took her hand in his, pressed his lips upon it, and, receiving her promise to think kindly of him, went away. His regiment was ordered to another part of the country, and into active fighting.

K   19

But the story had a happy sequel. In all the battles of the war the officer thought of Edith, and she, demure little Quakeress as she was, found that she loved him better than she knew. As soon as the soldier could honorably leave his master's service he resigned his commission and hastened to Long Island. He found Edith still "remembering him kindly," sweeter and lovelier than ever. By her gentle spirit she led him to become a worthy member of the Society of Friends, and rewarded him with a wife's devoted love.

THE LITTLE BLACK-EYED REBEL.

WHEN the British army occupied Philadelphia, the good patriots in the city were kept in complete subjection. The British officers, with their servants, had quartered themselves in all the best houses, and their constant presence and harshness of temper made it unsafe to express any sympathy with what they chose to call " rebellion." This was particularly unpleasant to the patriotic young women, whose warm hearts and impulsive natures had many a struggle with their fear of the unwelcome guests. All communication with the outside world was cut off, and the invaders told only such news as they pleased. Of course, the inhabitants soon found that no trust was to be put in the stories of unfailing success to the royal troops and constant defeat of the patriot army, with which the English officers took great pains to regale their ears on every possible occasion. It was too true that the soldiers of liberty were under a heavy cloud, and the prospect of independence was steadily growing darker. The great contrast between the appearance of the well-clad, well-fed troops of the king which came into the city and the ragged, overworked patriots who had marched out, was enough to give the keenest pain and fears to the sad spectators on that 26th of September, 1777. Yet victory sometimes came to the American arms; but even then it was well-nigh impossible for the patriots in the city to get the good news, and when they did they were afraid to show their joy. There were many Tories, however, in the place, and to these the royal officers usually told all that was going on at the seat of war. Many families were divided in their feelings, Tories and Whigs living under the same roof and eating at the same table.

In one of these families was a little girl whose name was Mary Redmond. Her father was a famous Whig, very active in his love for the good cause; but many of her relatives were loyalists and bitterly opposed to the revolution. Mary was a bright, sprightly child, full of life and wit, fearless and independent. She had very strong feelings about the war and she never hesitated to say what she thought, sometimes to the amusement, but oftener to the annoyance, of the British officers and their friends who were living at her home. Although these officers could control their tongues, they could not always control their looks and actions, and whenever any reverse had happened to their armies they were generally very harsh and unsociable. Towards the latter part of October, 1777, the officers quartered at Mary's house had shown one of these moods for several days, and the Whig ladies of the family were sure there was some good news for them, if only they could get hold of it. At last, one day, little Mary came running home, and with flushed face and quick breath burst out with the story of Burgoyne's surrender which she had just heard in the street. The good women's hearts leaped for joy, but in the presence of the English officers they dared not manifest it, warned by the black looks in their faces. Mary herself was frightened, but her delight was so great she felt she must shout or burst. She rushed through the group of angry officers, ran into the great deep fire-place, stuck her head up the chimney as far as she possibly could, and screamed at the top of her voice, " *Hurrah for Gates !*"

It is plain that so bright and fearless a spirit as hers would not be content with only shouting huzzas for her friends. As she heard so often from the lips of her hateful visitors the tales of suffering and defeat of the American soldiers, she burned to help them in their distress. How often she wished she were a man, that she might shoulder a gun and *do* something for her country! But if she had been a man she would have been powerless to help, with the city filled with the enemy, while very soon her innocent girlhood became the means of bringing great joy and relief to many a burdened and anxious heart.

The winter of 1777–8 came on, the terrible winter of Valley Forge. In that little valley on the banks of the Schuylkill the patriot army were staining the snow with blood from their unshod feet, and begging from day to day for food to still the cravings of sleepless hunger. In the city of Philadelphia the victorious British were sleeping in these patriots' beds, eating up their substance, and reveling in luxury and enjoyment. Within the city were the mothers and daughters, the wives and sweethearts, of many of the freezing, starving soldiers at Valley Forge; but no words of love and cheer could they send to the suffering ones in that terrible camp. Days and nights of agony rolled over these loving hearts, made worse by their unsuccessful attempts to communicate with their soldier-friends in the winter valley. The British were very watchful, and it was impossible for man or woman to pass their lines without permission, which was rarely given.

It was now that little Mary Redmond showed her courage and her wit. Sitting one day with her mother alone, she suddenly said,—

"Mother, I believe *I* can get letters to the soldiers, and back again, too."

Her mother looked up in astonishment. "Why, child, how can *you* do anything?"

"Why, you see," said Mary, eagerly, "there's a little boy comes in from the country most every day, and brings things to the market. I don't see how those ugly red-coats let him come in, but they do, and I know him; his name is Billy."

"But how do you know that he would help you?" asked the mother; "perhaps he isn't on our side."

"Oh, I found that out. He's a real good Whig, I tell you. I've played with him sometimes, and I like him."

Mary's mother smiled at her little daughter's eagerness and lively interest in the matter, but she knew too well her earnest and self-reliant nature to think lightly of her little plan, whatever it might be. So she said, playfully, yet meaningly, " Well, my 'little black-eyed rebel,' what do you propose to do?"

The child's outspoken sympathies had earned her this title from her Tory relatives, and she was by no means ashamed of it, for now, tossing back her little head with a saucy, defiant air, she exclaimed,—

"I just glory in that name, mother! and I'm going to show that it belongs to me, too. You see, I've thought this all over a lot, and I believe Billy can get letters from the camp, and hide them till he gets into the market, and then give them to me. It's going to be a good deal harder to get letters *out* of the city, but perhaps we can do it."

So the next morning the lively maiden set out gayly for the market. The streets were filled with noisy soldiers and drunken officers, and now and then she passed one whom she met every day at her mother's table. But this morning she did not stop to look at the brilliant uniforms or hear the fine bands play for drill. She tripped lightly along, all intent upon her wise little plan, and hoping nothing would happen to keep Billy from market on this day of all others. She did stop a moment when she got to the old Penn mansion, now filled with British officers, for Sir William Howe had just driven up to the house in Mary Pemberton's splendid coach, which he had stolen and used ever since he came to the city. General Howe was a noble-looking man, full six feet tall, and was well worth looking at in his gorgeous uniform and sur-rounded by a cluster of the highest officers in his army. But little Mary did not fall in love with any of these showy garments, for she considered them the badge of tyranny and cruelty.

" *Our* men are just as handsome if they *can't* dress so well, poor things!" she thought, as she went on her way; "and I'm sure they are a great deal nobler!"

When Mary reached the market it was all alive with people hurrying to and fro, or standing before

the stalls dickering for produce. Some fierce-look-
ing men, whose strange uniforms and outlandish
speech showed them to be Hessians, were drinking
beer and quarreling savagely over some dice at a
corner stall; and groups of officers here and there
stood smoking their pipes and talking about the
war. It nettled Mary to hear the word "rebel" so
often, and generally coupled with ugly oaths; but
she had become a little hardened to it from long
use, and her heart was strong in the faith that the
time would come when these hateful foreigners
would no more live on the fat of her land. Besides, just now her mind was full of her plan to
help her oppressed friends, and she could bear a
good deal without minding it so much.

She went straight to the stall where Billy always
brought his produce, and finding he had not yet
arrived, strolled nervously about, looking at the
various wares. She found a little picture of the
battle of Bunker Hill, and she thought it must
have been done by a Britisher, because it made the
royal army cut down the Americans by the hundreds. She got lost in thought as she looked at
the scenes of which she had heard such awful
stories at her mother's table, and was startled when
a merry voice shouted in her ear,—

"Halloa, Mary!"

She turned sharply, and seeing her friend, said,
with a laugh,—

K*

"Good-morning, Billy; how you scared me!"

"Did I? Well, you see, you looked like you was 'over the hills and far away,' as our milkmaid says. She's English, you know, but I like her though, first-rate. What are you looking at?" he added. "Oh, I see! Didn't we give it to 'em there, though! I'll bet——"

"Sh-h!" said Mary; "you must look out; the Britishers will hear you!"

"Well, there's *one* thing," said the boy, emphatically, "when I'm big enough *I'm* going to fight, too; and I'll bet I won't hold my tongue *then*, I tell you.

"Oh, dear!" said he, "I wish I was a man now! There's an ugly Britisher lives in our house, and I'd kill *him* the first thing.

"My folks say," he went on, "they'd rather have English gold than Yankee paper; but *I'd* rather have the paper, 'cause it *ours*, you see. We live better out to our house than we did before, but I'd rather be poor like we used to be, and not have such awful things to think about. Just think! that old red-coat at our house is always telling how many rebels he's killed, and says they stick 'em like pigs and——"

"Oh, dear!" shuddered his listener; "don't, Billy; I hear all about it at home, and it makes me feel sick. But I don't believe half they say, for mother says that they are awful liars. Come along, Billy," she added, tripping on; "let's go out."

"My father says"—Billy's tongue kept pace with his feet—"that I shall have to give fifty dollars for a jack-knife if our people beat, and have to bring two baskets to market, one full of produce and the other empty, so as to carry home two baskets full of money. But I don't care: I want to get rid of 'em; I hate to see 'em 'round. That old feller at our house is all the time cursing the country and the weather, and I got mad t'other day and asked him what he stayed here for, where he wasn't wanted, if he didn't like, and he called me a 'rebel brat.' I'll fix him for that some day, I tell you."

"It isn't half as hard for you as it is for me," said Mary; "for my poor father is out in that dreadful camp, and he can't get enough to wear or enough to eat, and we have everything nice. And he can't write to us, either." And the sweet voice trembled while the little black eyes filled with tears. Billy stole a look at the face of his friend, and when he saw the quivering lips and wet eyes, his heart swelled until it was as big as a man's. He put his arm around her, and felt strong enough to whip the whole British army.

"It's too bad, Mary," said he. "Don't cry! *Oh,* I wish I was a man! I'd kill every one of them!" And he almost screamed it out in his wrath.

"Oh, *don't* talk so loud, Billy. If the soldiers hear you they'll beat you. I saw them beat a little boy awfully the other day because he said, 'Hurrah for Washington!'"

The children had now got out into the square, and seeing a quiet spot where no one was standing, Mary drew her companion thither, and commenced in low, eager tones,—

"Billy, I think I know how you and I can help if we're *not* men."

Billy's eyes grew big. "Oh, wouldn't that be nice! How can we do it?"

"Why, you see, our folks are dying to hear from father, and we've got lots of friends whose men are in the camp, and I've thought you might send word to them, and they could send letters to you, and you could hide them and bring them in to me."

"Whew!" whistled Billy, "that's a big thing to do. I don't believe I could get by the lines with 'em."

"Do they ever search you?" asked Mary.

"Oh, yes, the ugly things! Sometimes they haul over the stuff; and one time they said I looked like a little rebel devil, and hunted all my pockets, and made me take off my cap, and shoes and stockings too." And Billy clinched his little fist at the memory of the insult.

"Oh, dear," said Mary, despairingly; "I'm afraid we can't do it."

Suddenly her face brightened, and, looking hastily around to see that no one was near, she exclaimed,—

"I've thought of a way, Billy. Couldn't you get the letters sewed into the lining of your jacket?"

" *Yes, sir*," said the boy, eagerly; "that's just the thing. The letters could be brought to our house, and mother would do it for me, 'cause she's a real good Whig, I tell you."

"You know you could have them stitched in kind of loose-like, so they would come out easy, only you musn't bring much at a time, for they would make a bunch."

So it was agreed that Billy should tell his mother at once, and get word to the poor soldiers at Valley Forge, telling them not to say anything important at first, till they saw how the plan would work. The two happy children separated, and Mary went home full of hope and joy.

It is not known how Billy contrived to communicate with the American camp; but his pluck and ingenuity won success, for a few days after the conversation he appeared again in the market, where Mary was anxiously watching.

After his business was done he strolled off with Mary to a retired corner. His face was very jubilant, and Mary felt he had good news, though she could scarcely wait to get out of hearing to know.

As soon as she felt safe she asked, almost breathlessly,—

"How is it, Billy? Tell me quick,—did you do
anything?"

"I'll bet I did," said the boy, proudly. "They're
right in the lining under my arm, where the jacket's
all loose, you know. They're just basted, and you
can rip it out easy with your finger."

Mary put her hand, trembling with excitement,
under the rough jacket, and in a moment her
fingers closed over the prize. She almost screamed
outright for joy, but thought of the consequences
in time to check herself, and only said, in low,
grateful, exulting tones, "*Oh, Billy!*"

The dear child wanted to fly now straight to her
home.

"Oh, Billy," she said, "I must run right back
as fast as I can. Just think how happy they'll
be!"

The little courier felt this was natural enough;
but he *did* want to play awhile, and just for a
moment he wished he had done nothing about the
business, any way. But the next minute he felt
proud to be able to make some sacrifice for his
country's good. He had heard a good deal about
this the past two years, and always thought *he*
would like a chance, and now he had it he accepted it bravely. It didn't come so easy, though,
as he used to think it would. Wholly taken up

with the rush of her own feelings, Mary did not suspect what was going on in her companion's mind; and soon, with hearty thanks and words of praise that sung in Billy's heart for many a mile, she said a loving "good-by," and hastened out of the market. Her heart flew on wings, but her steps never seemed so short before, and she thought there never *were* such crowds in the streets. She dodged in and out, got some rough words from a soldier against whom she tumbled in her haste, and never looked about her till she came to High Street. Here the way was blocked by thousands of soldiers passing in review before General Howe's headquarters. At any other time the brilliant, magnificent display and stirring music would have been a treat to the little girl; but now she stood nervously biting her lips, stamping impatiently with her tiny foot, almost crying with vexation. When at last the rear rank had gone by, she darted across the street, dodging her way between the crowds of teams that followed the soldiers, and, unable to restrain her eagerness, broke into a sharp run. A few moments later she rushed up the steps of her home, and her waiting mother caught her in her arms. The stoop and the hall were filled with officers smoking and gayly talking, and it was very necessary not to give them occasion to be suspicious. Some ordinary questions and answers about market matters passed between them, and Mary told of the review, while her mother went up to her chamber.

Soon the little girl quietly followed her, and, as the door closed and shut them into their safe retreat, she burst into tears and threw a bunch of letters into her mother's lap.

" Oh, mother, I hope there's one from father !"

Who can tell the eagerness with which that package was opened, the joy that filled the hearts of that group of loving women when the well-known hands appeared in the addresses, and for the first time in months they drank in the old-time words of tenderness and devotion? But there were letters for friends and neighbors, and Mary hastened, after the first flush of happiness was over, to take the precious missives to the waiting but unsuspecting hearts.

The next time Billy brought letters from the camp Mary took him to her house, and for the first time in his life he played the part of a hero, receiving, too, a hero's reward,—woman's love and gratitude. The ladies hugged and kissed him, and loaded him down with little presents, till at last his beaming face broke out from the midst of half a dozen arms all around him at once, and he cried,—

" *Won't* mother's eyes stick out when I tell *her !*"

Then they sewed into his jacket some letters for the loved ones at the camp, and with many earnest prayers for their safe journey and many blessings upon the bearer, sent him, joyful, on his way.

Thus the matter went on for several weeks, and the letters came and went with much regularity. But after a while it became evident that the officers in the house were growing suspicious and watchful. The boy's frequent visits, which always led to the meeting of all the ladies in Mrs. Redmond's chamber; the bright faces and joyful demeanor of the household after these calls, and especially the fact that some of the women occasionally let slip some bit of information which they could not have got in the city, all led the officers to mistrust that the boy was a spy. They followed him one day to the market, and learned that he came through the lines, bringing produce for the army. The good women noticed these suspicions, and when, one time, Billy told them he had been stopped at the lines and forced to strip, while all his garments were searched, they reluctantly advised him to come no more. Mary must go to the market and get the dispatches as she did at first.

But even here they were watched. Mary saw some of the officers who were living at her house strolling about through the square, always keeping in sight of her wherever she went. Greatly annoyed and troubled, she passed Billy at the stall, and said,—

"Look out! they're watching us!" Then she

turned back, and walked slowly by again, saying, hastily, " We'll play tag, and pretty soon you get as far off as you can and let me catch you."

In a few moments Billy stepped up suddenly, put his finger on Mary's shoulder, shouted, " I touched you last!" and darted into the square, hotly pursued by the little girl. Up and down they ran, Mary sometimes within arm's reach, and then losing ground as the boy put forth new efforts. Soon she dropped into a walk and looked slyly around. The officers were laughing at the chase, and although they were still looking on, she felt that their suspicions were vanishing, and she had strong hopes of succeeding in her deception. Billy had also stopped, and now, letting the girl get dangerously near, started off again at full speed. In and out they ran, dodging and turning on their tracks around the square. Mary's eyes were wide open, and when at last she saw the officers were walking carelessly about and not watching as sharply as before, she gained swiftly on the boy, and said, suddenly, " Now's the time!"

Billy ran off toward the farther corner, and slackened his pace enough to let Mary overtake him just as he turned to dodge. She pressed him against the railing, throwing her shawl over his head at the same instant. In a twinkling she slipped her hand under his jacket, tore open the seam, and grasping the letters, thrust them into her pocket. Then with light heart and light feet she darted up the square, chased by Billy, whose turn it was to pursue. Running up near the officers, and finding they attracted no attention, the pretended game was stopped, and the two friends separated, delighted with their success.

But although, after this, Mary succeeded by various devices in getting from the market boy the letters he brought, none could be given in return, and a few hastily spoken words from time to time were all the messages the suffering soldiers at Valley Forge ever received until the British army evacuated the city.

HOW THE CATTLE WERE SAVED.

ONE bright, breezy day in the autumn of 1775, a little sloop-packet was flying down the Delaware River, bound from Philadelphia to New Castle. The wind from the northward was fresh and increasing, and the crowded deck was lively with the shouts and laughter of the passengers, the gabble of fowls, piled coop above coop, and the blare of sheep, frightened at the rushing waters.

Not all the passengers, however, were merry; for while the young people had caught the spirit of wind and wave, full of life and glee, their elders were collected in quiet groups, sitting on coils of rope, or leaning on the weather-rail, and talking earnestly of matters which excited many disputes. But a few short weeks had passed since these men were suddenly startled by the wild news that Massachusetts had struck the first blows for American freedom, and their hearts yet echoed with the roar and boom of the cannon of Bunker Hill. Since the spring the dark cloud had grown steadily larger and denser; all ears were now filled with the rum-

ble of approaching war, and all eyes were looking
for the lightnings of actual conflict. But American hearts were sadly divided at the opening of
the great struggle, and while many supported the
Bay Colony in her resistance to tyranny, others
cared more for peace at any price. This difference
of opinion was found among the groups on the
little packet, and the discussion was gradually
growing high and strong.

The most earnest and able of those who spoke
for war was a young man of commanding form
and deep, earnest eyes, who was evidently a leader
among his fellows, as his words were listened to
with respect, and made a great impression upon
his hearers. This was Israel Israel, a man destined to become famous in the history of the
nation he was now striving to form. He seemed
to be about thirty years of age, and his sunburnt
face and able conversation showed him to be a
man of travel and experience with men. For the
past ten years he had been in the Barbadoes, and
having grown wealthy upon the island, had returned to his native land, and was now hastening '
to New Castle to his mother's home.

Against this gloomy background of war-talk
and dispute there was set in the young man's heart
a scene of joyous life and beauty. Upon a large
coil of rope in the bows of the sloop a bright cluster of girls had gathered, where, all facing inward,

they were chatting as only young girls can, and now and then bursting into merry shouts of laughter as a rough wave leaped against the little vessel and dashed the happy faces with the drops of the sea. One ringing voice from this frolicsome group had caught the young man's ear, and he closely watched the party till he learned which maiden it was whose heart seemed so full of the morning. She was the merriest of the merry, not yet seventeen, and of rare beauty of face and motion.

In the midst of this hilarity the hour drew near for dinner. The Delaware sloops made only short trips, had no cabin accommodations, and furnished no meals. Their passengers brought their own provisions, and ate as best they could, sitting or walking about the deck.

Aboard the packet the groups now separated,— the travelers ceased to talk and began to eat. Mr. Israel, thus left to himself, watched the young girl more intently than ever. She was gazing into the depths of a capacious satchel, and occasionally scanning the passengers on deck with a searching eye. Soon she rose, and, taking the satchel on her arm, came quickly aft. As she sprang over the coil of rope her lithe, graceful movement displayed to the watcher a foot and ankle of such beauty as he had never seen in all his tropical wanderings. At one step the little maiden had leaped into the stranger's heart. As she approached the nearest pacers on the deck, she courtesied with charming grace, and lifting the wide-open satchel, offered them her fare. Thus she went from one to another, distributing her dainties of bread and meat, of cake and tarts, till she reached the young man whose heart had beat louder and louder at every fall of the little feet. With scarcely a look at the stranger she presented her kindly offering. One glance into the satchel showed that her generosity had left scarcely enough for the giver's needs. Noticing his hesitation, the little maid looked up into his sunburnt face. As her eyes met his earnest gaze a bright, red flush flowed upward from her beautiful neck, and broke into ripples against the heavy masses of her hair.

"There is plenty for us both," said she, with that same wonderful laugh, only softer and stiller.

He drew forth a morsel, and, taking hold of the bag, said, tenderly,—

"Let me hold the satchel while you eat your own dinner. You deserve to enjoy it greatly after such generosity to strangers."

After a moment he added, "And what bright spirit must I thank for such charming courtesy?"

"Oh, I'm a little Quaker girl from Wilmington," said she, "and my name is Hannah Erwin."

And so the conversation went easily on, she very vivacious and winning, he feeling a glow in his heart that had never been there before. By a few judicious questions he learned that she belonged to an honorable family of Wilmington, that her ancestors came over with the good William Penn, and that she was returning from Philadelphia to a happy and loving household. The time passed so pleasantly that when at last the great mainsail flapped in the wind, he was surprised and disappointed on looking up to find the packet shooting in towards the Wilmington wharf. The young girl's friends were waiting her coming; and as her companion lifted her gallantly over the rail, a cheery word of thanks from her father gave the stranger a welcome glimpse into an honest and kindly nature.

He little knew what a tumult he had started in the maiden's bosom, and he was too much concerned with the new feelings which filled his own heart to give any thought, just now, to the condition of hers. He reached his home, but his stay was short. He could not rest till he had been to Wilmington. He went, was generously received by the good family, and shortly bore away with him a happy and beautiful girl, whose name had now become Hannah Erwin Israel.

One year and a half passed quickly over the young husband and wife, for without the times were full of stirring deeds, and within was perfect happiness and peace. Israel Israel had become a member of the Pennsylvania Committee of Safety, and the

little Quaker girl had developed a brave and reso-
lute heart that no one had expected to find beneath
her pure and sunny beauty. The times were very
dark for the struggling patriots. The British army
was now in Philadelphia; British vessels were in
the Delaware; and the *Roebuck* frigate was anchored directly opposite the Israel farm, a few
miles from the town of Wilmington. The farm
was small, and the house very modest, for the
young husband had lost all his fortune through the
vicissitudes of the war.

One night in this fall of 1777 the little wife
stood in the doorway of her home, anxiously
listening for the return of her husband. Having
learned the British countersign from a Tory neighbor, he had gone through the lines to Philadelphia on a visit to his mother and sisters, then living
in the city. While there he had been arrested by
a squad of soldiers, but succeeded, by his ready
wit, in deceiving his Hessian captors, and was now
hastening through the night to his waiting and
fearful wife. Back and forth, between her work
and the door, she flitted uneasily, her loving heart
filled with keen apprehensions, for she knew her
husband was a prize for which the enemy were
eagerly seeking. At last the well-known step was
at the gate, and as she sprang to her feet her husband stood beside her, safe once more by his own
fireside.

No, *not* safe! He had been betrayed! There was rushing of feet in the garden, a shout of strange voices at the door, and the room was filled with the glitter of British bayonets and the clamor of angry men.

"Not a word, sir!" commanded the officer, as he set his pistol against the breast of Israel, who was about to cry for help.

"Stand aside, madam! No time to lose!" for the devoted wife was clinging to her husband's neck, as if she could shield him from the coming doom.

"Not a step shall he go without me!" she cried passionately, and her eyes flashed upon the man who stood over her with drawn sword.

Enraged at the delay, the brutal officer shouted to his men, "Take her out of the way! Bind this man, and hurry him to the boat!"

The poor girl was rudely wrenched from her grasp and held by strong arms, while her husband was bound with cords. As the men dragged him from the room he begged her not to follow, as she could do him no good. On they rushed to the river, a mile away, thrust him into a man-of-war's boat, and bending to the oars with exultant strength, soon brought him to the *Rocbuck* frigate. Here he was treated with inhuman cruelty. As soon as he stepped on to the deck he was stripped of everything that the meanest sailor could covet; his watch

was taken; his heaviest garments were snatched off
from him, and even his silver shoe-buckles were
torn from his feet. Then he was hurled into a coil
of rope for a bed, and left through the night with
no covering from the wind and cold.

What a terrible night was that! He had no
hope of rescue; he knew a price was set upon
his head; and, as he glanced upward a moment
in prayer, he saw the yard-arm from which he
doubted not he should be hung before another sun
should rise and set.

Far in shore he could see the lights in his house.
Then it was he groaned aloud in his anguish. The
thought of his young wife, not nineteen years of
age, left alone to the mercies of war, was like a
knife in his heart.

After her husband was torn so rudely from her
arms and dragged out into the dark, unpitying
night, Hannah Israel sat awhile on the floor, where
she had been hurled by British sailors, with her
face plunged deep into her lap, and her heart crying out to God in its agony. Soon she looked up,
and the sight of her desolated home brought her
the sweet relief of tears. Thick and fast they
flowed; every tear, every sob, a prayer that reached
the ear that never slumbers nor sleeps. But she
was not one to give much time to useless grief,
and she presently rose and went about some household labor. The thought that her husband would

expect her to be brave nerved her heart now to a sturdy courage. The night was wearing on toward morning, and she longed for the light of day though she knew not that it could bring her any hope. Unconsciously, however, she was even now supporting the heart of her loved one; for after the first stabs of anguish at the sight of his home, the little beams from these far-away lights brought a strange peace to the prisoner's spirit. What might he not hope while yet the brave heart was so near him, and overhead the free sky of God? His soul grew quiet, for his trust was in Him.

The long-desired morning soon threw its quivering spears along the seaward sky. On board the frigate the prisoner, chilled with the dews of night, hailed its coming with joy, while ashore the first glimmer of dawn found the devoted wife straining her eyes to catch the outlines of the vessel that held all her hope and her life.

Early in the morning a sailor, pacing the deck, stopped suddenly before the prisoner and asked if he were a Freemason; learning that he was, the sailor told him that a lodge would be held in the officers' cabin that night, and the fact might be of some service to him. Here was a thread on which to hang a hope. Meanwhile, the prisoner's Tory betrayers had been active. While their victim was shivering on the inhospitable deck, they were carousing with the officers in their luxurious quar-

ters, and filling their hearts with enmity against
an honorable man. The revel was still going on,
though the sun was now over the taffrail. At
length a Tory said that Israel had often vowed he
"*would sooner drive his cattle as a present to General Washington than receive thousands of dollars in
British gold for them.*"

On hearing this the commander broke into a
rage of curses, and ordered the officer of marines
to send ashore a detachment of soldiers and
slaughter the cattle before the prisoner's eyes.
The officers and Tories went upon deck to see the
sport.

The boats were manned, the soldiers crowded
in, and soon the long sweeps brought them up to
the landing. The prisoner had watched these pro-
ceedings with increasing fears. What was their
point of attack? What would become of his wife?
But he was not long left in suspense. The soldiers
formed in ranks on the shore, shouldered their
muskets, and marched off toward a meadow, where
the cattle were grazing.

Other eyes had been watching this scene. Every
dip of those approaching oars had been felt in the
heart of the young woman, whose gaze was fixed
intently on the slowly-increasing forms, with a
faint hope that the dear one might be there. Now
the truth flashed suddenly across her mind. She
had no one with her in the house but little Joe,

who was only eight years old. Shouting to him
to follow as fast as he could, she darted out of the
house and flew to the meadow at the top of her
speed. She reached the fence, and tugged and
wrenched at the heavy bars. Just as she brought
them to the ground little Joe dashed up breathless, but brave.

" Quick, Joe! quick! fly down to the brook and
start those cattle this way!"

Off sprang Joe toward the river, tossing high the
dew with his little bare feet, and shouting, " Kole!
kole!" with all the strength of his lungs. The
young woman rushed toward the cattle that were
nearest the advancing soldiers, who, seeing the
rescue, were now coming on at the double-quick.

" Sho-o-o! sh-o-o-o! hi! go on!" she screamed,
as she wildly waved her arms at the lazy beasts,
and startled them from their dreamy cud-chewing,
lying here and there upon the turf.

" Keep away from those cattle!" shouted a voice
from the advancing enemy.

" Hi-i-i! get up! go on! go 'long!" cried the
little woman; and she flew like an arrow from
group to group, stinging the stupid cattle into life
and haste by her clarion calls.

Joe was now coming up from the brook, driving
his herd toward the bars on the keen run. The
whole field was in motion; the two droves had
met and were plunging on toward safety, hotly

pursued by the friendly drivers. The soldiers had reached the lower fence, and were leaping over into the field.

"Stop there! let go o' those cattle!" cried the British officer, as he alighted on his feet in the field.

On ran beasts and drivers, unheeding the command.

Again that voice came up from the meadow, angry and harsh, "Stop driving those cattle or I'll fire!" For the first time the brave young girl stopped and turned. She looked down the hill and saw the red-coat soldiers rushing up at full speed, their bayonets and gun-barrels flashing in the morning sun.

"*Fire away!*" she shouted; and turned again to chase the herd. There came a crash of muskets from the meadow, and the bullets shrieked and hummed about her head. (Oh, the wild heart on the frigate's deck!) The terror-stricken cattle reared and plunged and fled wildly about the field. The lithe form leaped after them with fiery impulse.

"Head 'em off! head 'em off, Joe! drive 'em in!" she screamed, and the nimble feet once more turned the beasts toward the bars. Volley after volley came up from the on-rushing troops; the bullets screamed through her hair and plowed the ground up about her feet, or buried themselves in the rails of the fence. She heeded them not!

The cattle were leaping through the bars, and riding over on each other's backs. Little Joe had fallen beside the fence, and lay paralyzed with terror as the howling bullets struck the rails over his head. As the last beast rushed into the lane, the daring young girl reached the bars, and dragging the helpless boy through by the hair, swung him on to her arm with unnatural strength, and flew on toward the house. She drove the bellowing herd into the barn-yard and fastened the gate upon them with her own little hands. Then, pursued by a parting volley from the cowardly soldiers, she entered the house and sank exhausted with fatigue and the terrible excitement of the chase. But the cattle were saved !

Baffled by the courage and spirit of a mere girl, not daring to enter the farm-yard for fear of the rallying neighbors, the heroic soldiers of the crown returned to the boats and the ship amid the jeers of their watching comrades.

On board the *Rocbuck*, Israel Israel was now forced to turn from his young wife's peril to his own. While yet his heart was overflowing with gratitude at her escape, though fearing still that she might have been wounded and the boy carried off slain, he was summoned to trial before the enraged officers of the ship. On entering the cabin, he found them seated around a table, dressed in full uniform, and with black looks of hatred and

vengeance in their faces. His Tory accusers were
there. In answer to the charges, the prisoner confessed his journey to Philadelphia on the night of his
capture, but denied that he had gone on any secret
service, as the visit was solely to carry aid to his
mother and sisters who were suffering want. He
acknowledged, too, that he had often said he would
drive his cattle as a present to the American camp
or destroy the whole herd rather than sell them
for British gold. At this point of the trial the
prospects of the patriot were very gloomy. His
Tory neighbors pressed him savagely, and showed
the most unrelenting hatred. Suddenly, out of
this cloud of impending doom, the prisoner flashed
the Masonic sign upon the commander's sight. It
was returned!

From this moment everything was changed.
Significant glances passed round the table; the
threatening looks vanished from the British faces,
and the fierce tones softened into tenderness. The
trial was continued a few moments for the sake of
appearances, when the prisoner was acquitted, and
the court broke up, after bestowing upon the Tory
betrayers the most scathing rebuke for seeking the
destruction of a noble man. The officers crowded
around the young patriot, and warmly took his
hand; they praised him for his courage and for
his filial love; they did him honor for his fearless
answers in the face of an ignominious death; while

L*

the disgraced Tories, cowering beneath their bitter contempt, like whipped dogs slunk away out of sight.

In the little house on shore, the heroic young wife sat by an open window, gazing with yearning eyes upon the British frigate. The excitement of her wild exploit had passed away, and now the shadow of that terrible ship lay heavy on her heart. What a beautiful sight it was! How calmly and peacefully the vessel lay upon the shining river! for the day was still and breathless, and the stream flowed on without a ripple. But the watcher knew it was a creature of death, and she feared it was to her a ship of doom. Those long spars had a terrible fascination to her! Who could tell but any moment might see the loved form shot up to that black yard-arm? She had more than once known the British troops to hang a patriot before his very door!

Suddenly there was a great commotion on the, frigate's deck. Over the bulwarks she could see the gleaming of bayonets rushing to and fro. Had the fatal hour come? Soon the men were seen streaming down the ship's side and entering a boat. It was not a long-boat, nor a man-of-war's boat, for it had an awning! It left the great black shadow, and the long sweeps stretched away toward the shore.

Hark! A wild blare of trumpets,—and a soft

strain of bewitching music floated over the still waters to her car!

Was it all over? Had they come to bury him? Then the trumpets broke out into riotous joy,—the ringing notes chased one another merrily about; in the midst of the jubilee the barge reached the landing.

With dazed mind and trembling limbs the young wife tottered to the door, and gazed toward the river. The soldiers formed in marching order, and the glittering ranks were now moving toward the house. Again the trumpets burst into joy! A group of officers led the troops, followed by sailors bearing a load. In the midst of the officers walked a tall man in a military cloak. She shaded her face with her hand, and for one moment threw her whole wild soul into her eyes! *It was he!*

The proud little wife sprang from the doorway and flew down the lane. The whole glorious truth burst upon her soul at once!

From such a scene the officers turned their faces in tender respect. The sailors laid upon the stoop their burden of rich silks and costly gifts; the squad faced about, and the music soon grew faint in the distance.

A HEROINE IN PINAFORES.

SEVERAL attempts were made during the war to capture General Schuyler, and in the summer of 1781 the Tòries determined upon one more desperate effort to get possession of their hated enemy. John Waltermeyer, a fearless loyalist, collected a band of followers, and, going stealthily to Albany, lay concealed for many days in the pine shrubbery around the general's house.

They waited long before they could get any knowledge of the general's situation. At last, one day, a Dutchman who worked for Schuyler came through the pines. The Tories sprang upon him and dragged him to their hiding-place. Under threats of instant death they made the poor man give a full account of the approaches to the great house, the situation of the sleeping-rooms, the habits of the family, and all the facts which could aid their dark plot. It would not do to murder the Dutchman, or to keep him a prisoner, for this would arouse suspicion of their presence.

They set him free after forcing an oath from him that he would tell no tales.

The honest man, however, hastened to his master and related the whole story. General Schuyler at once fortified his place, and set a guard of six men over the house, three by day and three by night.

It was now August, and the dog-star ruled over Albany. The desperate Tories and Indians in the pines were cursing the heat, the mosquitoes, and the long delay.

Within the high garden-walls the great stone mansion looked placidly down upon its besiegers with an air of security and complacency which was most exasperating. The sun was drooping low through the trees, but seemed to give its last shots with unusual spitefulness, for the heat was greater than at noonday.

The three night-guards were in the basement, and had not yet awoke from their day's sleep. The men on duty were conquered by the intense heat, and were lying at full length in the cool grass, far down the garden. A married daughter of the general had collected the sentinels' guns, which were left lying about, lest the children should be injured,—a deed which soon caused the capture and imprisonment of three brave men.

The general sat in the broad front hall, beside his beautiful wife; the children moved quietly

about; and in the open nursery the little babe
Bess slept in the cradle, for the peace of approaching twilight filled every heart.

Meanwhile, the enemy without were not idle.
Unable to bear the heat in the pines, and trusting
that the sentinels would be off their guard, the
Tories and Indians moved cautiously up to the
garden entrance and hid under the wall. Waltermeyer pulled the garden bell.

A servant now entered the hall, and announced
to her master that a stranger waited to speak with
him at the back gate. The trick was seen; the
general sprang to his feet; in a moment all was
confusion. The doors of the house were instantly
shut and barred. Seizing the children, the parents
rushed to the upper story; the general then ran
to his chamber for his arms. He looked out of
the window; the house was surrounded with
men. The guards must be aroused and the town
alarmed; he threw up the sash and fired his pistol.
He then ran up-stairs to his family.

The children rushed to their father as he entered.
Perhaps the little boy remembered the morning
when he opened the door upon the captive Burgoyne and his officers, as they awoke in his father's
house, and shouted, "You are all my prisoners!"
Wee Margaret was terribly frightened. The men
were heard breaking in the door below, and filling
the house with wild tumult.

Suddenly the mother turned deathly white; she sprang to the door with a loud cry.

"Oh, my baby! she is in the cradle!"

The general caught her in his arms, and held her with fierce grip. She struggled passionately.

"Oh, general, our baby!"

"You must not go!" he said, firmly; "you cannot save the child, and you will be murdered!"

Little Margaret had ceased her wailing. There was now a look on her face too strong and high for her years; but she had the best blood of the province in her veins. She slipped behind her father and opened the door. An appalling uproar came up from below,—the breaking of furniture, the shrieks of servants, and the savage shouts of the assailants. Above all this she heard a small, dear voice crying feebly and piteously. It was her baby sister.

There was no fear now; she was every inch courageous. She remembered a little prayer, and leaped forward. A strong arm stretched out to hold her, but she was gone.

Father and mother caught a glimpse of her streaming hair as she whirled around the upper landing, and then a deep stillness filled that little room; not a sob was heard, for every heart was lost in prayer.

There was one who remembered the words He had once spoken, that he who loseth his life for another, shall save it, and his eye was upon the brave girl. She saw men in the chambers as she flew past the open doors, and at the head of the lower flight stood a fierce savage. But her heart did not quail; she dashed by. Below her she saw the angry men breaking open the great chests of silver, and quarreling over their prizes. She heeded nothing, for she no longer heard the baby's voice, and a terrible sickness came over her heart.

"What had happened? why did it not cry?" Her knees almost gave way, but she rushed desperately past the painted savages and into the room.

The sweet little babe was quietly sleeping. Amid all the uproar an angel of God must have soothed it again into slumber.

With a wild shout of joy Margaret snatched the infant from the cradle and sped toward a private staircase. Just as she reached the foot an Indian hurled his tomahawk at her. The savage weapon cut off a piece of her dress a few inches from her head, and buried itself in the balustrade. God's shield cannot be pierced by tomahawks!

Margaret bore the baby swiftly up the stairs. At the landing a great, rough man stood before her, —it was Waltermeyer, the leader. He thought she was a servant: God blinds the eyes of the wicked.

"Wench! wench!" he cried, "where is your master?"

"Gone to alarm the town!" replied the child, as cool as she was brave.

Waltermeyer was frightened. He rushed below. The ruffians were plundering the dining-room. He hastily called them together for consultation. Just at this moment General Schuyler raised the window in the upper room, and shouted in loud tones, as if speaking to a large number of men, "Come on, my brave fellows! Surround the house and secure the villains, who are plundering!"

The robbers below heard the shout, and tumultuously fled. The quick ears in the chamber heard little feet rushing along the upper hall. The next moment Margaret laid the baby in her mother's arms, and fell, sobbing, across her mother's knees.

22*

THE MAIDS OF FORT GRISWOLD.

At daybreak of September 6th, 1781, the startled people of New London looked out from their chambers upon a fearful sight. Twenty-four British vessels covered the beautiful waters before the town. The alarm spread like fire, the town was at once aroused, and messengers rode at head-long speed into the country to call the militia for defense.

It was not a moment too soon. The great fleet loomed up against the town and lowered its boats, which were speedily filled with men. The doomed inhabitants saw the terrible array of scarlet uniforms and gleaming steel drawing rapidly near; men rushed hither and thither to meet the foe, while the air was filled with wailing of women and children and the boom of alarm-guns.

The fleet of small boats divided; about eight hundred men under Lieutenant-Colonel Eyre landed on the Groton side of the Thames, and the same number set out for the town itself. As these drew nearer, the terror-stricken watchers saw the

form of the traitor Arnold leading this savage band
of Tories and Hessians against his native State.

Very few militia-men had yet assembled, and
these strove vainly to prevent the landing. The
defenses on the New London side were so feebly
garrisoned that they could not be held against the
enemy; the advanced battery was first deserted,
then the little band left Fort Trumbull and crossed
over to Fort Griswold, on Groton Hill. The town
was now at the mercy of the foe, and they had not
come to show mercy, but hate. Suddenly a cloud
of smoke rolled up from the wharves. They had
fired the town! The people rushed to save what
they might out of their homes, but it was too late.
The flames leaped from house to house with fearful rapidity. The wretched inhabitants fled to the
open country, whence they gazed with breaking
hearts upon their ruined homes. There were other
eyes looking upon the frightful scene with de-
moniac delight. They were the eyes of Benedict
Arnold, who stood in the church belfry to witness
the desolation which he was making almost within
sight of the house in which he was born.

But another sight more terrible than burning
homes now attracted the weeping eyes without
the town. The enemy across the river had formed
in battle array, and were marching toward Fort
Griswold. The wailing ceased, and a speechless
anxiety seized upon the women, for every one had

some loved soul among the little fort's brave defenders.

Amid the tearful group were two young maidens whose hearts were now trembling with the first heavy sorrow they had known, but whose names should arise out of this day's ashes to immortal fame. Fanny Ledyard was the niece of Colonel William Ledyard, who was commanding the little fort now awaiting so silently the enemy's charge. Beside her stood Anna Warner, who had left home that morning with her uncle, when the alarm-guns rolled their dreadful sound across the peaceful fields, and was now watching with strained eyes the narrow walls which held her relative and her boy-lover, for Elijah Bailey was among the defenders, though but seventeen years of age. The militia had flocked in from the country, and now made a rush upon the burning town. Arnold saw them from his belfry, and, hastily descending, fled to his boats.

Meanwhile, the force under Eyre had crept cautiously through the woods and captured an advanced redoubt. The British leader then sent a white flag to Colonel Ledyard, with summons to surrender. The brave little garrison instantly refused, although some had no weapon, and many were armed with pikes alone. Several hundreds of people had gathered within sight of the fort, and the commandant sent an officer to implore them for aid,—for recruits, guns, ammunition. Colonel Ledyard trusted to this expected help when he refused to surrender; but he looked in vain. The wretched officer got drunk, and in that glass of liquor were drowned the lives of many noble men.

The British now rushed to the assault. The rattle of musketry and the shouts of men pierced the ears of those praying women, already deafened by the roar of flames behind them. For nearly an hour the battle was fierce and loud. The fort's flag was shot away very early in the fight, and tender eyes watched in vain to see it replaced.

Young Bailey had been sent before the assault to man a gun at an advanced redoubt, with orders to retreat if he could not hold the post. The British charge was so· fierce that everything fell before ·it. The boy opened upon them with his cannon, but as the glittering wave of steel came on it was evident the redoubt must fall. Elijah's comrade fled to the fort, but the brave boy stopped, in the teeth of the on-rushing foe, to spike his gun. Then he started for the fort, but when he reached it the gates were locked and he could not get in. Bitterly disappointed not to bear a hand in the battle, he would not flee to the rear but laid under a fence close by, where he could witness the whole scene.

The half-armed garrison defended the works

with such bravery and skill that the British were repulsed at every charge and finally turned to flee to their boats.

A great light sprang up in those watching hearts across the river, only to die down as suddenly into utter darkness.

The British rallied for one more charge. With the fury of desperation they hurled themselves upon the pickets. The stakes gave way. With fierce shouts the troops rushed over the parapet in the face of a terrible fire, and fell upon the garrison with their bayonets. After a short, hot struggle the fort surrendered. The British commander was wounded, and soon died. Major Montgomery was transfixed with a pike. Bromfield then commanded, and, while his troops still fired upon the unresisting Americans, he demanded of Colonel Ledyard, "Who commands this garrison?" "I did, sir, but you do now," replied Ledyard, at the same time surrendering his sword to Bromfield. The British miscreant snatched it from his hands and immediately ran his prisoner through with it. Thus perished a noble man by the hand of a most infamous wretch.

This was the signal for a massacre, which for diabolical wickedness has never been surpassed.

"Kill every man! don't let one escape!" cried a wounded British officer, his dying eyes wild with hate and revenge.

When no man was left to oppose them the victors plundered the fort. Then they collected many of the wounded, and, placing them one above another in a wagon, drew them to the edge of the hill, and launched the cart down the steep bank toward the river. The fiends stood at the top to see their victims drown. As the clumsy cart tore down over the rough hill-side the cries of agony wrung from the dying men were heard by that distracted group of women beyond the river,— heard far above the roaring and crackling of the flames and the fall of burning houses. Who was now a widow? who was an orphan? who, perchance, had lost her all? No tongue can tell of the prayers that were hurled against that hill-side to block the wagon's descent.

At last an apple-tree caught it and held it fast. Shouts of joy went up from the women, and shouts of rage from the demons on the hill. They rushed down to the wagon, but the remainder of their wrath God restrained. They lifted out the crushed and bleeding men. Some were dead, many were dying. Some they paroled, the rest were stretched upon the ground and left to their fate. The dying men begged piteously for water, but, although there was a well in the fort, not one was allowed a drop to drink.

As darkness settled upon the scene, the British gradually withdrew to their ships. Through all that terrible night the women sobbed and prayed in agony. No one dared cross the river, for it was not known that the enemy had left. The few whose homes were yet standing gave shelter to the homeless. Young Anna Warner returned to her country home, three miles from town.

With the first ray of morning, Fanny Ledyard was creeping cautiously through the woods toward the fort. Fearful of meeting the enemy at every step, she yet could restrain her heart no longer. It was still dark in the woods, but on the outskirts the birds had caught the glimmer of dawn, and were shaking out their songs into the cool air. The trees, too, had their delicious morning fragrance, and the wild-flowers were dewy-sweet.

But neither song nor fragrance could now waken any response in the pure heart of this ministering angel. Above all the morning joy rose the pungent smell of smoke and the groans of the wounded.

As the maiden drew nearer she heard distinctly the piteous cries. Some called for water, some for death; many dying lips were pleading the name of some one near and dear; many were beseeching God to take their souls.

With bursting heart the young girl stepped in among the outstretched forms. At the sound of her feet men moved their heads with agony, and as they saw, through the dim light, the form of the maiden stooping tenderly over a fallen comrade, some cried out in their delirium that it was an angel from heaven, and some that God had sent His spirit to take them home. A hundred arms stretched out to her in terrible appeal; unnumbered wounds besought for healing.

Her dainty feet were wet, and her heart sickened as she thought that it was human blood; but she moved on in the strength of Love and Mercy. A chill of horror crept over her when she laid her hand upon an upturned face and found it cold; but she passed quickly to the next, and brought a gleam of light and joy to the closing eyes.

The noble girl had come not only with her heart full of love, but with her hands full of gifts. She brought water and chocolate and wine. Now she poured the refreshing draughts down the parched throats, tenderly holding each languid head upon her knees, and bathing the face with cold water from the well. She was soon recognized, and her name passed reverently from dying lips to dying lips again. She spoke gentle words of trust and cheer; she told the tortured souls of their loved ones who would soon be here. As she moved on, the cold, half-opened eyes of her noble uncle stared stonily up to the broadening light of day. With a shudder of terror and a swelling heart she stooped to close the lids, and then passed hurriedly to those who were not beyond relief.

Voices were soon heard in the woods, and she found herself alone no longer. People flocked rapidly in from the town and the fields, all bearing needed mercies in their hands,—food and drink, bandages and lint. Surgeons came, too, and began rapidly to dress the wounds.

Among the foremost of the new-comers was Anna Warner. Her lover and her uncle had been in the fort, and with distracted heart the young girl left her home at daybreak and flew to the fatal spot. Her lover was soon beside her, unharmed. A clasp, a kiss, a fervent cry of gratitude for this greatest mercy, and the two separated to search for the uncle. Soon the maiden found him stretched upon a cot in a neighboring house, whither he had been carried. His wounds had been dressed, but his eyes were fast losing their light, and it was evident that death drew near with rapid step. Anna bent over him, and with feeble voice he pleaded for one last look at his young wife and little babe. The brave girl felt that a sacred trust had been given to her. With a kiss, and gently charging the failing man to cling to life till she could return, Anna sped from the house.

Now the young limbs stretched themselves to a desperate race. Death was hastening on nimble feet; could she get back to her uncle before the dread angel should come?

For more than three miles she ran at full speed,

never stopping for breath. She dashed into the house and gave hurried orders to the stricken wife. She flew to the field, caught the horse, saddled him, and brought him to the door. Then she lifted the delicate, sick wife upon the beast, took the babe in her own arms, and started back afoot.

The young mother put whip to the horse and dashed down the road. She was soon out of sight, but Anna put her whole strength into the struggle. She was sorely burdened now, this girl of seventeen, and once, as her limbs nearly failed her, she almost determined to give up the contest. He would have his wife beside him soon, and it would not make so much difference about the child. Ah! but he asked for *wife and child*. Again the girl threw all her energies into the race. Even now death might be entering his door!

Over field and ditch, through woods and thicket, flew the noble girl, with the precious burden in her arms. She reached the house, she entered the room. The dying arms were unclasped from the wife's neck that the little babe too might be folded in that last embrace, and the heroic maiden turned her face to the wall in tears of bitterness and of joy.

ANECDOTES.

Just before the outbreak of the war handbills were thickly posted around New York, calling on the people to take up arms and shake off tyranny. The British authorities were unable to discover how these handbills were put up. It was done by a little boy, who was carried in a box strapped to a man's back. The man would lean against a wall, as if tired,—and the lad drew back a slide, pasted on the poster and shut himself in again. Watching his opportunity, the man moved on to another place.

In the fall of 1775, some boys in Queens County, Long Island, having caught a number of cats, went out on to the plain with horses and dogs, for the cruel sport of hunting poor pussy. The first bag was opened and the cat sprang out; the dogs leaped after the cat, while the boys followed on horseback. The chase led toward Hempstead. It happened that an assemblyman, a Tory, was taking an airing on the edge of the village. He saw the great cloud of dust, and then the horsemen plunging, furiously onward. The Tories had been for weeks fearing a descent upon them by the patriots across in New England. The Tory fled into the village at the top of his speed, shouting, "The Yankees are coming!" The place was in an uproar at once. People snatched up what they could take most easily and fled. They hid in barns, old cellars,—in every dark place. There they waited long hours, expecting to hear the shouts of the foe and the crackling of flames. Everything remained still. At last a few bold ones ventured to peep about; then they stole out, and soon all had slunk, thoroughly ashamed, to their homes. A valiant justice ran so far, when the alarm was given, that he did not get back for three days !

The story of General Gage and the Boston boys is well known. Enraged at the tyranny of the troops, they called upon the general. "We come, sir," the leader said, "to demand satisfaction." "What !" exclaimed the general, "have your fathers been teaching you rebellion and sent you to show it here ?" " No one sent us," replied the lad, while his face flushed at the word " rebellion"; "we have never injured or insulted your troops, but they have trodden down our snow-hills and broken the ice on our skating-grounds. We complained, and they called us young rebels, and told us to help

23*

ourselves if we could. We told the captain, and he laughed at us. Yesterday our works were destroyed for the third time, and we will bear it no longer." The general was struck with the spirit of the lads. "The very children here," said he, "draw in a love of liberty with the air they breathe;" and he dismissed the boys with the promise that their rights should henceforth be protected.

At the commencement of the troubles, Governor Wentworth, of New Hampshire, took refuge in the fort at Portsmouth. At the first opportunity he fled to Boston. But many of the patriots believed he was still hidden in the fort, and a party one day entered the quarters and asked permission of Mrs. Cochran, the commandant's wife, to search the rooms. They hunted in vain, and then asked for a light to examine the cellar. A bright little daughter of Mrs. Cochran's cheerfully offered to light them. She held the candle very well until the searchers had got into a distant part of the cellar, thickly set with beams, when she blew out the light and ran up-stairs. She soon heard them knocking their heads against the beams and swearing desperately. The little rogue called out in the sweetest and most innocent tones, "Have you got him?" The only answer she received was some remarks not very complimentary to the "little Tory."

WHEN the British fleet approached to seize New York, in 1776, their coming was first discovered by a girl, Nelly Cornell. She lived in a house at Far Rockaway, and looking out of the window, she cried to an American officer, "I see trees rising from the ocean!" The Americans withdrew at once.

THROUGH all the time Long Island was held by the British, a Tory neighbor kept carting manure from the stables of a Mr. Creed, and using it for himself. But a little daughter of Creed's took it upon herself to keep account of the loads, and after the war she brought out her paper, and the Tory had to pay for every load.

A COMPANY of lads, mostly riggers and boatmen, called "Moulder's Boys," did noble service in New Jersey. They took Washington's army across the Delaware on that famous passage, and fought bravely at Trenton and Princeton.

WHEN our army retreated from Ticonderoga, in 1776, a little son of Colonel Cilley, named Jonathan, was accidentally left behind. When the British found who he was, they took him to Burgoyne. The general treated him kindly, and gave him his liberty, telling him he might select for himself any article he wished from the captured baggage. The little fellow took the finest regimental coat he could see, which proved to belong to Major Hull, who was afterward general. Burgoyne also gave the boy an old horse and a pair of saddle-bags which he filled with copies of his famous proclamation. When Jonathan reached his father, Colonel Cilley was in front of his regiment on parade. The boy gave him a handbill. The father read it, then tore it in pieces and scattered it about, exclaiming, " Thus shall his army be scattered!"

WHILE the British were encamped at White Plains, in the fall of 1776, the people suffered much from the depredations of the troops. A garden belonging to a widow had been frequently robbed by night. She had no protector, but one day her son, a little boy, asked permission to catch the thief. He got a loaded gun and hid himself in some bushes in the garden. Presently a British soldier, a great, tall Highlander, came along and deliberately filled a large bag with fruit, swung it to his shoulder, and started off. The little fellow sprang out, and with cocked gun threatened the man with instant death if he should drop the bag. In this way the boy drove the Highlander before him all the way to the American camp. When the soldier had put down the bag, he turned to look at his captor. An expression of intense disgust came over his face, and he cried, " A British grenadier taken prisoner by such a —— brat! such a brat!"

In Woodbridge, New Jersey, one morning of March, 1777, a girl happened to pass an empty house, when she saw, through the window, a drunken Hessian soldier, who had strayed from his ranks. There was no man upon whom the girl could call within less than a mile of the town. She hurried home, dressed herself in male attire, and, taking an old gun, hastened back to the house. The man was still there. The girl went boldly in, and, aiming her gun at the Hessian, forced him to deliver up his arms. Then she drove him before her toward the town, when a patrol guard of Americans came along and she turned her prisoner over to them.

After Fort Montgomery was taken by the enemy the dwellers along the Hudson felt unsafe. A Mr. Belknap, living near Newburgh, sent his wife and children back into the country in charge of his son, who was but sixteen years of age. Young Belknap soon returned to the old home, and, finding his father was away in the army, the boy took the sashes from the windows and removed the remaining furniture and buried all in the woods. This was to make the house appear deserted, so the British should not molest it. He then went

M*

back to his mother. But soon he heard that the enemy were coming up the river. He could tend his sheep no longer, but hurried off to Newburgh. On the way he borrowed a gun and bayonet and ammunition. He flew about—collected a dozen or two more boys, and they all hastened to the river-side. When the lads reached Newburgh some boats filled with British troops were opposite the village. As the transports tacked and came near shore, the boys fired from behind some trees. The enemy answered by cannon-shot. This warfare was continued every time the British neared shore, for several hours,—the boys' shots producing much confusion on board the transports. At last the wind changed and the enemy sailed beyond range.

At Tarrytown, on the Hudson, stood the old Dutch mansion known as Wolfert's Roost. In 1777 the British fleet lay in the broad river opposite the house. Old Van Tassel, the owner, had pierced the walls with loop-holes, for the building stood on the " Neutral Ground" and was constantly liable to attack. His only garrison was his wife and his sister, Nochie Van Warmer, said to be "a match for the stoutest man in the country." The sturdy Dutchman was often away from home, pursuing the enemy with his immense goose-gun, which was his only piece of ordnance. During one of these expeditions a British armed vessel came into the bay and anchored close by the Roost. A boat-load of men came ashore and approached the house. The goose-gun and its owner were away, but the wife and the stout sister and the negro woman flew to arms at once, seizing whatever was handiest for a weapon. Besides these, there was the daughter, rosy-cheeked Laney Van Tassel, "the beauty of the Roost." These brave defenders made a terrible onslaught with brooms, shovels, and fire-tongs. But the enemy succeeded in plundering the house, and when they left they caught up the blooming Laney and hurried her toward the boat. The women shrieked and pounced upon the marauders. It was a desperate fight all the way to the river, when an officer on the frigate shouted to the men to drop the girl, and she escaped.

In the spring of 1777 a fierce attack was made by British and Indians on the house of Moses Pierson, in Vermont. The battle was most desperate and lasted for hours. Two of the defenders were Pierson's sons, Ziba and Ural, seventeen and fifteen years of age. A baby slept through the struggle unharmed, although a number of balls were found in the bed and several went through the head-board. The two boys were soon after captured and taken to Montreal, where they were thrown into jail. The prison was directly over the St. Lawrence, and when the river had frozen over the lads escaped. It was night, and a light snow had fallen, which would clearly show their tracks. They crossed the river and entered the woods. Here they crossed and recrossed their tracks, reversed their shoes, walked back part of the distance, and finally hid in the forest. Just after daylight a large party rushed by their hiding-place in hot pursuit. The boys kept hidden until the third night; then they set forth cautiously toward Lake Champlain. They traveled only by night at first, hiding during each day. They had nothing to eat but what they could find. They had no guide but the sun, which was often obscured. When they had been journeying for twenty-five days they found in the forest the log cabin of a lumber-camp. The boys hid near by until the workmen had gone forth in the morning. Then they approached the house stealthily. They found only an old man, drunk, and fast asleep. One stood over the old man ready to kill him if it should become necessary, while the other collected provisions. They got safely away with as much as they could carry. When they reached the lake they crossed to their old home, after forty days' suffering, and found it deserted and desolate. A few frozen peas and potatoes were lying about, and the famished boys ate them greedily. They pushed on, and were soon welcomed by their parents, — nearer dead than alive, reduced to skeletons by their year's adventures.

In one of the skirmishes on Long Island a Colonel Webb was taken prisoner, with many of his soldiers, and among these a little fifer of the smallest size. When the colonel was called before the British general, the fifer-boy followed him closely, anxious to know his commander's fate. As soon as the general spied him out, he asked, in astonishment, "Who are you?" "I am one of King Hancock's men," said the little fellow, bravely. "Can you fight?" asked the general. " *Yes, sir*, I can!" The royal officer called in one of his own fifers, and said to King Hancock's little man, "Dare you fight him?" " *Yes, sir!*" The general ordered the lads to strip, and the little Yankee fell so furiously upon the red-coat that he was speedily demolished. His friends were obliged to rescue him. The general was so pleased with his little enemy's pluck that he gave him his liberty at once.

During a British raid into New Jersey, in May, 1778, the officers stopped to dine at the house of Francis Hopkinson, one of the signers, who was absent at this time. A young girl named Mary Comely came in from a neighboring house and got the dinner for the British. While the officers were dining, the girl discovered that the soldiers were plundering the houses of her mother and grandmother across the street. She rushed into her home, crept up on tiptoe behind one of the thieving men and cut a piece from the skirt of his coat. She showed this to the commanding officer, who thus caught the offender and his comrades, and the plunder was restored.

GEORGE MAUN, a famous Tory, much dreaded by the Whigs, was discovered hiding in a wheatstack by a young patriot of sixteen. The boy would have brought him down with his gun, but yielded at last to Maun's pleadings,—because he had been kind to the lad's father,—and allowed him to escape to the mountains.

AT the beginning of the battle of Monmouth General Washington, surrounded by a large staff, rode toward Monmouth Court-House. Suddenly a little fifer-boy dashed up, and very quietly said, "They are all coming this way, your honor." "Who are coming, my little man?" asked General Knox. "Why, our boys, your honor, and the British right after them," said the little fifer. "*Impossible!*" exclaimed Washington, in consternation, as he dashed his spurs into his horse. It was the first news of the dire rout.

IN 1782, the house of John Burtis, on Long Island, was attacked by whaleboatmen. David Jervis, a young lad, defended the place, while Mr. Burtis loaded the guns, and his wife, Molly, handed the powder. The assailants were driven off, the boy having killed their captain, whose watch, gun, and clothes were given to the lad. He had once before saved the house from destruction.

WHEN the house of John Mitchell was assailed, his little boy, Benjamin, came down-stairs just as the ruffians broke in. One of them seized him, asking, " Do you know me?" " Yes," said the unwary boy. Finding they would be detected, the man replied, " Then you shall never know me again," and took the little fellow out and shot him.

GENERAL PUTNAM captured some Tories and prepared to hang them. On the day of execution the hangman could not be found. Two boys, about twelve years old, were ordered by the general to hang the culprit, and notwithstanding their tears they were forced to obey, at the point of the sword. It was necessary to punish the Tory for his evil deeds, while if his executioner was a boy there was less danger of retaliation on the part of the man's friends.

WHEN the British approached Elizabethtown,

New Jersey, Governor Livingston fled from home, leaving his valuable documents in a trunk under charge of his young daughter, Susan. As the troops drew near, she stood upon the roof of the piazza to look at them. A young officer rode up and besought her to go in for fear she should be fired upon. Susan attempted to climb in at the window but found she could not. In an instant the horseman was by her side and gallantly lifted her through. On being asked to whom she was indebted, the officer replied, " Lord Cathcart." The young lady then asked protection for the box, which contained, she said, all her private papers, and the obliging officer set a guard over it, while all the rest of the house was sacked. The girl's coolness had saved the State papers.

A YOUNG lad once saved Alexander Hamilton from an unpleasant adventure. During the winter at Morristown, young Hamilton, then colonel and aide to Washington, was paying court to a daughter of General Schuyler. In his evening visits to Schuyler's headquarters, the lover was accustomed to take with him a little son of Mrs. Ford, at whose house Washington made his quarters. Returning from a visit one evening, Colonel Hamilton had missed the lad, and, as he reached the lines and received the guard's challenge, became confused and could not remember the countersign. He could think of nothing but "Miss Schuyler." The sentinel held his bayonet to the officer's breast, and Hamilton began to feel much distressed, when he heard little feet pattering towards him through the darkness. It was the boy. Taking him aside, Hamilton asked him in a whisper for the countersign, and, having learned it, returned to the sentry and was allowed to pass.

AT the destruction of Wyoming, Mrs. Skinner fled with six helpless children, the youngest but five years old. Amid the keenest suffering these poor little ones walked with their mother all the way to Connecticut, three hundred miles, and much of it through a savage country. The thrilling story of their perils and pains would fill a book.

ONE of the most romantic incidents in all history is connected with a child of Wyoming. A little girl, five years old, was stolen from the valley by Indians. After the war closed, her brothers visited the Indian countries to discover any trace of her, but were unsuccessful. Fifty-nine years after she was stolen, she was found by a brother living as queen among the Miamis in Indiana. She had forgotten her native tongue, but not the loved ones of her childhood.

ON one of Brandt's invasions along the Mohawk,

the savages rushed to a schoolhouse, determined to exterminate a whole generation at one blow. The teacher was killed and some of the boys were tomahawked, while others hid in the woods. The little girls ran wildly about, shrieking with horror. Brandt rushed to them and painted a black mark on each apron. He told them to hold up the mark when the Indians came near and they would pass them by unharmed. The shrewd little girls at once called out the boys, and daubed each one with black paint. So all were saved.

BRANDT was very merciful, for an Indian. At the attack on Wyoming, he caught little Mary Whittaker by the hair and painted a red mark on her face, so that she was spared. At the same time he saved the life of a child, John Finch, whom some Indians were about to tomahawk because he had laughed at their queer looks.

THE farm of Mrs. Van Alstine, in the Mohawk Valley, had been robbed of everything by the Indians. As winter came on the sufferings of the family were so intense that it was determined to recover their property or perish. The brave son of Mrs. Van Alstine, but sixteen years of age, went with his mother to the Indian village, and in the face of the tribe recovered their household goods and cut the horses loose, bringing them all home safely.

ONE evening in March, 1780, a little fellow of fourteen or fifteen, named Chauncey Judd, had been making love to pretty Ditha Webb, in Waterbury, Connecticut. While he was making the most of his little love's society some Tories had been robbing the store of Ebenezer Dayton, a rich patriot. Chauncey left the house late, and after he had got partly home, was met by the robbers fleeing with their booty. As he knew some of the men they took him prisoner and dragged him on with them, fearing that, if allowed to go home, he would expose them. The country was soon aroused and the pursuit was hot. Several times the poor boy was told to prepare for death, while the leader of the gang stood over him with loaded gun. But each time something interfered to save his life. In one of their hiding-places, Chauncey's father passed so near that he could have touched him, but the boy dared not speak for fear of instant death. At length, after long wandering and terrible suffering, he was rescued. As the gang slept a drunken sleep one night, the pursuers rushed in upon them and captured all but one. Chauncey's sufferings had been so great that for a time his reason was impaired. But he recovered and lived to old age.

THE "WIDE, WIDE WORLD" SERIES.
The Works of the Misses Warner.

The Wide, Wide World. 12mo. Two Steel Plates. 694 pages. Fine cloth. $1.75.

Queechy. 12mo. Two Illustrations. 806 pages. Fine cloth. $1.75.

The Hills of the Shatemuc. 12mo. 516 pages Fine cloth. $1.75.

My Brother's Keeper. 12mo. 385 pages. Fine cloth. $1.50.

Dollars and Cents. 12mo. 515 pages. Fine cloth. $1.75.

Daisy. 12mo. 815 pages. Fine cloth. $2.00.

Say and Seal. 12mo. 1013 pages. Fine cloth. $2.00.

☞ *Complete sets of the above volumes, bound in uniform style, can be obtained, put up in neat boxes.*

The sale of thousands of the above volumes attests their popularity. They are stories of unusual interest, remarkably elevated and natural in tone and sentiment, full of refined and healthy thought, and exhibiting an intimate and accurate knowledge of human nature.

THREE POWERFUL ROMANCES,
By Wilhelmine Von Hillern.

Only a Girl. From the German. By Mrs. A. L. WISTER. 12mo. Fine cloth. $2.00.

This is a charming work, charmingly written, and no one who reads it can lay it down without feeling impressed with the superior talent of its gifted author.

By His Own Might. From the German. By M. S. 12mo. Fine cloth. $1.75.

"A story of intense interest, well wrought."—*Boston Commonwealth.*

A Twofold Life. From the German. By M. S. 12mo. Fine cloth. $1.75.

"It is admirably written, the plot is interesting and well developed, the style vigorous and healthy."—*Boston Saturday Evening Gazette.*

TWO CHARMING NOVELS,
By the Author of "The Initials."

Quits. By the BARONESS TAUTPHŒUS. 12mo. Fine cloth. $1.75.

At Odds. By the BARONESS TAUTPHŒUS. 12mo. Fine cloth. $1.75.

What a Boy! Problems Concerning Him. I. What

shall we do with him? II. What will he do with himself? III. Who is to blame for the consequences? By JULIA A. WILLIS. With Frontispiece. 12mo. Fine cloth. $1.50.

"Every member of the family will be sure to read it through, and after enjoying the author's humor, will find themselves in possession of something solid to think about."—*New York Christian Union.*

"There is a vein of practical sense running through the story which will be food for old and young readers, and the charming love scenes render the book one of absorbing interest, and the reader must be dull enough not to relish the book from beginning to end."
—*Pittsburgh Commercial.*

The Nursery Rattle. For Little Folks. By Anne L.

HUBER. With Twelve Chromo Illustrations. Small quarto. Extra cloth. $1.75.

"'Nursery Rattle' is all the better because it generally does not pretend to carry meaning or moral with it, and it has a musical ring in it."—*Philadelphia Inquirer.*

"The best collection of nursery songs from one pen in the language. Simplicity of idea, clearness of expression, brevity of words, and fine humor and sympathy mark the 'Nursery Rattle.'"—*San Francisco Alta California.*

Diana Carew; or, For a Woman's Sake. A Novel.

By Mrs. FORRESTER, author of "Dolores," "Fair Women," etc. 12mo. Fine cloth. $1.50.

"A story of great beauty and complete interest to its close. . . . It has been to us in the reading one of the most pleasant novels of the year, and at no time during our perusal did we feel the interest flagging in the slightest degree. . . . Those who admire a love-story of good society, and who especially admire ease and naturalness in writing and character painting, will find in Mrs. Forrester's latest novel a deep pleasure."—*Boston Traveller.*

Pemberton; or, One Hundred Years Ago. By

HENRY PETERSON, author of "The Modern Job," etc. 12mo. Extra cloth. $1.25.

"As a historical novel this work is a graphic representation of the Philadelphia of the Revolution, and as a romance it is well imagined and vividly related. The interest never flags; the characters are living, human beings of the nobler sort, and the style is simple, chaste, and appropriate."—*Philadelphia Evening Bulletin.*

"The style is graceful, fluent, and natural, and the various conversations between the different characters are marked with strong individuality."—*Philadelphia Ledger.*

Alide. A Romance of Goethe's Life. By Emma

LAZARUS, author of "Admetus, and other Poems," etc. 12mo. Fine cloth. $1.25.

"A charming story beautifully told, having for its subject the romance of a life, the interest in which is and must for a long time be intense and all absorbing."

"This is a tender and touching love-story, with the best element in love-stories, truth. The story is very charmingly told, with rare grace and freshness of style."—*Boston Post.*

The Livelies, and other Short Stories. By Sarah

WINTER KELLOGG. With Frontispiece. 8vo. Paper. 40 cents.

"It is a long time since we have read a more agreeable or better written book. The authoress has a pleasant, racy, lively style, considerable powers of humor, and at times of pathos."—*New York Arcadian.*

"'The Livelies' is a sketch of domestic life made thrilling by the introduction of incidents of the great fire at Chicago."—*Philadelphia Age.*

"The tales are pleasantly written, in a bright, taking style, both the plots and characters being interesting. The book is decidedly readable, and will assist materially in hastening the flight of an odd hour."—*Easton Express.*

"There are five admirable stories in this book, all well told and interesting."—*Baltimore American.*

The Fair Puritan. An Historical Romance of New

England in the Days of Witchcraft. By HENRY WILLIAM HERBERT ("Frank Forester"), author of "The Cavaliers of England," "The Warwick Woodlands," "My Shooting Box," etc. 12mo. Fine cloth. $1.50.

"It is a stirring story of stirring events in stirring times, and introduces many characters and occurrences which will tend to arouse a peculiar interest."—*New Haven Courier and Journal.*

"The story is a powerful one in its plot, has an admirable local color, and is fully worthy to rank with the other capital fictions of its brilliant author."—*Boston Saturday Gazette.*

"The story is well and vigorously written, and thoroughly fascinating throughout, possessing, with its numerous powerfully dramatic situations and the strong resemblance to actual fact which its semi-historical character gives it, an intensity of interest to which few novels of the time can lay claim."—*Philadelphia Inquirer.*

"A romance of decided ability and absorbing interest."—*St. Louis Times.*

The Green Gate. A Romance. From the German

of Ernst Wichert, by Mrs. A. L. WISTER, translator of "The Old Mam'selle's Secret," "Gold Elsie," "Hulda," etc. *Fifth Edition.* 12mo. Fine cloth. $1.75.

"It is a hearty, pleasant story, with plenty of incident, and ends charmingly."—*Boston Globe.*

"A charming book in the best style of German romance, redolent of that nameless home sentiment which gives a healthful tone to the story."—*New Orleans Times.*

"This is a story of continental Europe and modern times, quite rich in information and novel in plot."—*Chicago Journal.*

Patricia Kemball. A Novel. By E. Lynn Linton,

author of "Lizzie Lorton," "The Girl of The Period," "Joshua Davidson," etc. 12mo. Fine cloth. $1.75.

"'Patricia Kemball' is removed from the common run of novels, and we are much mistaken if it does not land Mrs. Linton near the skirts of the author of 'Middlemarch.'"—*Lloyd's Weekly.*

"The book has the first merit of a romance. It is interesting, and it improves as it goes on. . . . Is per-

haps the ablest novel published in London this year."—*London Athenæum.*

"'Patricia Kemball,' by E. Lynn Linton, is the best novel of English life that we have seen since the 'Middlemarch' of 'George Eliot.'"—*Philadelphia Evening Bulletin.*